THE ENEMY OF MY ENEMY IS NOT
ALWAYS A FRIEND.

THE DAR

WAR ZA

BOOK ONE OF T

KSIDE

ARY BROWN

SAGA  PRESS

LONDON SYDNEY **NEW YORK** TORONTO NEW DELHI

ICARUS CORPS

SAGA PRESS + An imprint of Simon & Schuster + 1230 Avenue of the Americas, New York, New York 10020 + This book is a work of fiction. Any references to historical events, real people, or real places are used fictitiously. Other names, characters, places, and events are products of the author's imagination, and any resemblance to actual events or places or persons, living or dead, is entirely coincidental. + Text copyright © 2015 by Simon & Schuster, Inc. + Jacket illustrations copyright © 2015 by Steve Stone + Icarus Corps logo by Craig Howell + All rights reserved, including the right of reproduction in whole or in part in any form. + SAGA PRESS and colophon are trademarks of Simon & Schuster, Inc. + For information about special discounts for bulk purchases, please contact Simon & Schuster Special Sales at 1-866-506-1949 or business@simonandschuster.com. + The Simon & Schuster Speakers Bureau can bring authors to your live event. For more information or to book an event, contact the Simon & Schuster Speakers Bureau at 1-866-248-3049 or visit our website at www.simonspeakers.com. + The text for this book is set in Bembo Infant. + Manufactured in the United States of America + First Edition + 10 9 8 7 6 5 4 3 2 1 + Library of Congress Cataloging-in-Publication Data + Brown, Zachary. + The Darkside War / Zachary Brown. — First edition. + pages cm. — (The Icarus Corps ; Book one) + Summary: "For ages, people have looked at the stars and wondered if we were alone in the universe. Now we damn well wish we were . . . There are many aliens out there. They come in all sorts of shapes and sizes. You will probably fight besides creatures that will haunt your nightmares long after you leave the service, and they're the good guys. However, if you want to survive your first encounter with the enemy there are five aliens that you need to learn to spot on sight. Pay attention now and you might live to see your mama again someday. These are the enemies of the Accordance. Our enemies. They are the Conglomeration, and they seek to destroy us. So we will destroy them first. Devlin Hart becomes part of an irregular army for an alien civilization. A reluctant recruit, he's only here because his parents have been captured by the alien Accordance. Devlin will have to decide where his real allegiances are: because the enemy of the enemy is not always a friend. In this case, they're a far, far worse threat"— Provided by publisher. + ISBN 978-1-4814-3035-7 (paperback) — ISBN 978-1-4814-3036-4 (ebook) + 1. Human-alien encounters—Fiction. 2. Science fiction. I. Title. + PS3602.R726D37 2015 + 813'.6—dc23 + 2014048849

THE DARKSIDE WAR

1

I stood at attention. My boots dug into the sad, scraggly patch of open field that was all that remained of what had once been called Central Park, and I remembered standing in the middle of a baseball field here, once. A long time ago.

Shit, I had to have been, what, three years old?

Our ragged lines formed up between the organic mangrove-like legs of alien spires. The matte-black, treelike structures dwarfed the human-built New York City skyscrapers: our glassy, blocky, primitive efforts to reach toward the sky.

A human sergeant in Colonial Protection Forces gray, a single red shoulder stripe marking his rank in the Accordance, walked up to face the lines of human recruits.

"Listen up, you useless maggots," he shouted, his voice amplified so much it hurt my chest and left my ears ringing. "There are many aliens out there. They come in all sorts of shapes and sizes. You will probably fight beside creatures that will haunt your nightmares long after you leave the service, and they're the good guys."

He paused a moment to let that sink in. Some of those

"good guys" watched us from balconies that jutted out like dark thorns from the slender legs of their buildings, but from down on the ground they were just a collection of distantly tiny, odd shapes to our eyes.

"However, if you want to survive your first encounter with the enemy, there are five aliens that you need to learn to spot on sight. Pay attention now, you might live to see your mama again someday."

The human sergeant held up a black-gloved fist. He raised an index finger.

"Drivers: They're cat-sized and scaly. Those pronged rear feet will sink into the flesh of your back and hook on. That pink ratlike tail? Once it plunges into your spinal cord, you're a brain-dead meat puppet at its total and utter disposal. Ever see a whole squad turned into zombies for the enemy? You will."

Two fingers up. I shifted and wiped the sweat from my forehead. Something like cinnamon wafted through the cool air from one of the nearby portals leading inside.

"Trolls: Yes, they look like rhinoceros that stand on two feet. Either of which could stamp you into a puddle of human goo. That armor? Nothing short of depleted uranium gets through it. I've seen one of these flip a tank. Ever come face-to-face with one, you call in an air strike and run like hell."

Three fingers.

"Raptors: Our enemies decided that a velociraptor with a brain, thumbs, and the running speed of a cheetah wasn't good enough, so they made cyborgs out of them. They also carry rifles. But they smell like chicken if you hit them with a laser."

He smiled when he said that, and held up a fourth finger.

"Crickets: These insectile robots are the first wave. The winged variants provide air support as well. Shoot them to bits. But watch out, those twitching leftovers reassemble as needed. So make sure the bits are really, really tiny, and then shoot them some more."

He uncurled his thumb. His voice changed. More serious. Lowered. I leaned in slightly.

"And lastly: Ghosts. They seem to be in charge, the masters of it all. We think they're covered in advanced adaptive camouflage. They stay out of the fight, and any nearby enemy forces will sacrifice themselves in a suicidal frenzy to protect a ghost. So if you see one, kill it. If you can. No one has ever survived a face-to-face with one; we just get the suit recordings afterward."

A gaggle of civil servants in dark-blue uniforms spilled out of a portal and milled around in clumps, watching us. Three orb-shaped cameras flew overhead, hanging in the air as if gravity were just a minor annoyance as they recorded us.

This was a show, and I knew it: Watch the recruits line up and get processed. I would be on any number of news streams and live shows.

"These are the enemies of the Accordance," the sergeant shouted. "These are *our* enemies. They are the Conglomeration, and they seek to destroy us. So we must destroy them first. We will teach you how. Do you have any questions?"

Yeah, I thought. How long will any of us survive against that?

The sound of chants and protest floated between the buildings: fifty or so licensed protestors in a permit-cleared free-speech zone on the edge of the Accordance Administrative Complex.

Last week, there had been tens of thousands of them.

+ + + +

The protest against alien occupation grew around the edges of the gnarled forest of alien structures. Summer heat beat down, refracting off the windows and buildings, and the determined, angry crowd smelled of sweat, body odor, and street food. Tents lined the sidewalk and spilled onto the street, creating a haphazard fabric city. Barrel fires filled the air with a sharp-tasting haze.

Some thousand people had elbowed me in the ribs or stepped on my feet before I stopped, suddenly transfixed by a pretzel cart along the Harlem side of 110th. Four men in suits on the other side of the Harlem antiterrorist gates eyed me warily as I sidled up to the cart and breathed in the smell of fresh pretzels.

"Devlin?" The voice came from behind a pair of protestors in gray hoodies holding up two halves of a broken globe and waving them in the air.

"Devlin Hart!"

I frowned. I knew the voice. I knew that the caller's name started with a *T.* But I'd been in four different schools just in the last year and a half. My parents kept moving from safe house to safe house.

"Tristan, right?" I asked.

"Yeah!" Tristan ducked under the fractured globe easily and sidestepped people to get closer to me. We'd played soccer. He was a striker, I remembered. Up at the front, compact and fast. He moved through the crowd like he slipped between players on the field: quickly and efficiently. He held a quad-copter drone in one hand.

"What are you doing here?" Tristan asked. And then he laughed as we grabbed hands, half shook. "Right, I didn't mean *here,* at the protest. I meant here in this part of the street. Figured you'd be near your family."

I soaked up the moment of familiarity. I'd liked the three weeks I'd gotten to play on a team. Make some friends. Before my family had been forced to move and hide again. "We're on a food strike."

"That sucks."

"Yeah. No one asked me if I wanted to join." I was just, it seemed, the son of Thomas Hart. *He* was the Great Planner. The leader of the closest thing humanity had anymore to a resistance.

What was a little hunger compared to the Fight? The Fight to get humanity back out from under the thumb of the overlords that had descended from the skies before I was born. That from orbit had destroyed the cities of the world that rose up against them.

"You're protesting?" I asked.

"Recording." Tristan grinned. He held up the quadcopter. "Watch." He threw it into the air. The four propellers buzzed and it hovered in place above us, waiting for instructions.

Tristan circled it around overhead a few times using his phone to pilot it. "A few friends of mine rented a room nearby; we've been flying these things and streaming the video all over. Drop a few ads in, we've been making some spare cash. Everyone's curious to see who blinks first: protestors or Accordance enforcers." He nodded toward the nearby gate leading into Harlem, where the businessmen still stood and stared at the crowds. The gates slid down into the ground and under the sidewalk.

Two struthiforms in lightweight armor walked out in front of the businessmen. Fast and dangerous, they looked like stoic ostriches dressed in ancient Roman armor. But the heavy Accordance-made energy rifles held across their feathered chests in scaly arms were nothing but serious.

"Jesus," I said. Usually the enforcers carried stun guns and prods for protests. These looked ready for war.

The sound of the crowd changed around us. The chants and hive-like buzz of protest shifted, like a changing wind, and built into a low growl as people noticed the escorts.

"Go home," shouted a woman in baggy jeans as she shoved an Earth First poster with a hand-painted version of a simplified, almost cartoonish green globe at the two aliens. The suits behind the guards grimaced and stepped back slightly. The struthiforms moved their feathered hands into the oversize trigger guards of their rifles and stepped forward.

The vendor slammed the windows shut over his hot plates, balled up his apron, and slid into the cab of the rolling cart. My stomach grumbled. The cart rolled away with a whine as the vendor piloted it gently through the crowd and down the crowded street.

The woman with Earth First poster stepped right in front of the struthiforms, her placard high in the air as she blocked their way onto the street.

"Step aside," the struthiform on the left said, voice strong and authoritative via a translation collar on its spindly neck. I could just barely hear the hisses and clicks of its natural language underneath the human voice the collar projected.

"You have no right to order me to do anything."

The standoff created an island of tense silence as people watched the birdlike alien confront the human protestor.

The struthiform on the right hit her in the stomach with its rifle butt, forcing her to double over. Leaning back on one massive leg, the alien pinned her roughly to the ground with the other. The flattened talons grasped her waist as she struggled to get free. The struthiform aimed the rifle at her head. "You will cease your obstruction, or face a penalty," the struthiform said.

Members of the crowd shouted back, anger bursting into the air. More faces turned toward us.

"Quick," I hissed at Tristan. "Buzz them."

"What?"

"Buzz the drumsticks, before the crowd turns on them. Remind the enforcers they're being watched. Live. Or they'll kill someone."

"They might come after *us*."

"Then give me your phone."

"No. No, I'll do it." Tristan swooped the drone down low, skimming above the crowd and stopping it just above the aliens. The fans blew air downward, ruffling the struthiforms' feathers. They glanced up and the one on the left raised its rifle.

A snap of light, pure energy leaping outward from the rifle's barrel, melted the drone right out of the air.

Tristan swore and looked around, ready to run.

But the distraction broke the tension. The struthiform on the right let go of the woman. She wriggled away, leaving her poster on the ground and keeping her hands in the air, her defiance blunted by the show of force.

The struthiforms took the moment to continue through the street, escorting the suited humans toward the midnight-black forest of alien buildings on the other side. Off to do whatever it was civil servants did for Accordance bureaucracy in there.

"I'm sorry about the drone," I said, taking a deep breath of hot air tinged with smoke. I held back a cough.

Tristan shook his head as if it were no big deal. But his hands shook a little as he rubbed them together. "It's okay. They're disposable. I have a couple more."

I swallowed. "I can pay you back." I actually couldn't.

Tristan shook his head. "I'm going back to get another one, but I don't think I'm coming back out into the crowd. It's changing, isn't it? I want to catch it, live. But I should leave."

"Okay." The San Francisco riots had been put down bloodily, so I understood his reluctance to get caught in the middle of something going bad. The New York chapters had practiced discipline. I'd helped train some of the cells. You had to convince people to not raise a finger in the face of violence, to take the beating that would come when enforcers came out with stun guns.

You had to drill them hard to stand in place, militarily, and not flinch. And despite the instincts deep inside you, you could not fight back. Because when you did, like they did in San Francisco, the Accordance had the excuse they needed to use more than nonlethal force.

That discipline didn't come easily to human beings. We could get pissed and riot. We could murder each other. Blow things up and run away. Rage was easy. But calm defiance: tough.

Tristan hesitated. "Hey, if you want, I have some food back in our room. Not a good view of the protest, but we can launch drones. Want to come meet everyone?"

My stomach clenched and gurgled. The press of humanity around us had slipped from celebratory to hostile. Even just pushing through it to get back to the organization tents I was supposed to be hiding in seemed a little dangerous.

"If it turns negative," my mother had whispered to me after San Francisco, "don't worry about me and your father. You get out before the enforcers start creating a line."

Something neither of us had told my father she'd said. Our little secret.

I was already on the fringe, why not get a little more

distance just to be safe? And get something to eat. I'd never promised to be part of their hunger strike.

And I half suspected the hunger strike was bullshit. For a month we'd been huddled in a Yonkers slum, living in a tent not much fancier than the ones pitched on the street here. Since San Francisco, donations to the cause had dried up. We could barely afford food right now.

"I'll come," I said.

We snaked out along 110th, ducked up one of the few ungated North Harlem streets, and got away from the dull roar and heat of bodies. The number of humans faded as we moved farther into Accordance space.

A few more struthiforms in armor moved along the streets. Heavy Accordance security. Human cops in duckling-yellow uniforms followed the struthiforms like little hatchlings, as ordered. We steered clear.

I followed Tristan up the stairs of an old brownstone converted into a hotel advertising housing for "All Species." Two floors up, and then into a corridor where the doors seemed to lean slightly and the fluorescent lights flickered shadows onto the wall. He knocked three times on the door to room 305.

The moment the door cracked open, Tristan bolted inside.

"What are you—"

I ate the following words. Two struthiforms in full midnight-black armor stood in the empty room. They looked at me, dinner-plate-sized eyes not blinking behind their armored visors.

"I'm so sorry," Tristan said from behind them.

"You asshole!" I shouted as he disappeared out the window and down the fire escape.

I spun around to run and came face-to-face with the

compound eyes of a carapoid. The horse-sized beetle of an alien didn't have any armor. It didn't need it. Its bony wings snapped out, filling up the corridor and knocking plaster from the walls. "Surrender peacefully," it warbled.

I scrabbled backward. Another carapoid grabbed me. Its sticklike arms wrapped around my chest and protuberances dug hard against my ribs as it lifted me off my feet into the air.

"Cease struggling," a struthiform standing behind me shouted.

The carapoid twisted and slammed me against the wall to make the point. Breath knocked out of me, my head swimming, I nodded and wiped blood from my nose.

"I'm done."

The carapoid dropped me to the ground, and a struthiform put scaly claws to the back of my neck.

"Devlin Hart, you are to be detained under the Human Antiterror Act 1451-B. Resistance will be met with mortal force."

The other struthiform roughly zip-tied my hands behind my back.

2

I rattled the shackles holding my wrists to the table in the middle of a sterile oval room. Two chairs flanked the table I sat at. Ovoid screens displayed deep ocean water and the room was filled with a faint bubbling sound. A contrast to the simple chain-link holding cells I'd been tossed into outside the building along with hundreds of other protestors swept up in the last several hours.

The door opened. The man in the black Armani suit screamed lawyer. He moved like lawyer. Smiled like lawyer.

"You're not Stephan," I said suspiciously. "Where's my family lawyer?"

The man sat across the table from me. He crossed his hands and gave me the considered, serious look. It came down like a mask, along with a mildly patronizing, lecturing tone. "I'm Gregory Stafford, and I'm your Interceder, not your lawyer. We don't have lawyers anymore, Mr. Hart, you should know better. And I'm assigned to you because there's a conflict of interest in your being represented by your previous Interceder."

"I've been standing inside a chain-link cell for three hours,"

I said. "In the sun. It's too small to sit or lie down in, and too hot to lean against the metal. I want Stephan. I have the right."

"The right?" Stafford looked pityingly at me. "You have no *rights*, Mr. Hart. You are involved in an act of sedition during war. Your parents are due to be executed, and you'll be lucky to be back out in that cage if everything goes well."

I tried to jump out of my chair. I shouted at Stafford, and my manacles crackled with electricity. My back wrenched straight and every muscle in me clamped down hard enough that I tasted blood.

My head struck the white table as I fell forward. I lay slumped, drooling out of the side of my mouth, every muscle in my body screaming.

Stafford leaned forward so he could meet my stunned gaze. "The Accordance has been waiting for the right moment over the last few years. All the while, it has been modeling how best to stop threats to recruitment. Now, all over the world, movements such as your father's have been raided and rolled up. There is no more antioccupation movement. Tomorrow morning, live broadcasts will show leaders of movements and cells being executed for treason. Your question, Devlin, is how you survive the next few hours."

"Tegna Gnarghf," I spat as best I could, still trying to get feeling back into my checks as I moved my jaw around.

"What's that?"

I took a deep breath and tried again. "Tentacle licker."

Stafford's high cheekbones reddened. "Listen, whether you like it or not, the Accordance came here. They have superior weapons. They destroyed DC. They took Manhattan. They sit in every major world capital. We've ceded them the moon, and other planets because we've never even reached them. And in exchange for that legal grant, we get some autonomy. The fact that, under their agreement to follow *some* human protocols, you're considered a minor and will not die with your parents: That's all that keeps you alive. Time to shape up, now, Mr. Hart."

I could sit up now, though the room wobbled and spun around me. I rubbed my eyes and groaned as I tried to process all this. From betrayal to capture. Everything turned upside down so fast. My father had organized peaceful protests, not fought on the streets. This was protest, not the damn Pacification. "What . . ." I gritted my teeth. "What do we do?"

"There are some options." Stafford tapped the table, and documents appeared on the surface. "The main concern the Accordance has is that they're in the middle of a war. It was why the Accordance was even created: defense. And they need recruits. You understand about the war, right?"

"Yes." I rolled my eyes. "We hear it all the time. About the Conglomeration. I've seen the propaganda. Five different species allied against the Accordance." Hopefully Stephan was meeting with my parents right now, trying to think of ways to stop all this. My heart hammered against the back of my throat, and it wasn't just because I'd been zapped. Everything settled onto me like a horrifying weight, trapping me in my chair. You knew the Accordance rule from on high. But then you encountered their boot on your throat, and it was suddenly too real.

"Against us all," Stafford corrected me. "The Accordance protects us. Anything that hurts recruitment, risks lives. Our lives. And your family, Mr. Hart, has risked many. However, recruitment is voluntary. The Accordance understands the value of good public relations. I think I can help you make a case to Accordance judges that executing a minor would be a horrible PR decision on their part."

"But not my parents?" I whispered.

"Just you. I'm sorry." Stafford's lawyerly mask slipped for a moment. I fought to keep seated and still, not wanting another muscle-clenching explosion of electricity to leap through my body.

I slumped farther down into my chair. "The only reason I won't die is because they don't want the bad PR."

"The war out there is real," Stafford said. "Even if it hasn't come to our world yet. If we're lucky, it won't. The Accordance needs fighters. From everyone it protects. We stand together under the Accordance umbrella, or we'll fall to something far worse. So they are being very careful here."

I couldn't imagine something worse than the Accordance. Something that destroyed cities from orbit and marched through the ruins in black power armor, ferreting out the remaining resistance with overwhelming force.

But there was apparently something out in the universe that made the rulers of the Accordance, the squid-like Arvani, shit their tanks. Even if no one on Earth had ever seen it.

And now my parents were going to die because of it.

"My father thought peaceful resistance would work," I told Stafford. "My parents saw what happened during the occupation; they thought this was a better path."

"The Accordance is ruled by aliens, not humans," Stafford said. "The Arvani and the Pcholem do not tolerate dissent, violent or peaceful. And the other species have less power within the Accordance. Your father should have known this; he was jailed for his inability to follow guidelines when teaching Indigenous Mythology."

Indigenous Mythology. My dad taught History 101 at NYU before I'd been born. He still insisted on carrying the old pre-occupation textbooks, big paper-printed monstrosities, around with us as we moved from house to house.

I blinked my eyes several times and looked away. I was so angry with them right now. Angry for spending my childhood never staying in one place. Angry because they always felt there was a higher purpose in their lives, a purpose far higher than anything I could ever mean to them.

What was a child compared to the past glory of humanity that had once ruled itself? I knew my place in the world. In my parent's world.

This was their fault, I thought angrily. *They'd* chosen this. It certainly wasn't my fault. Fuck, I was still hungry because of their choices. Even if I got out of this room, all I had was a hot, smelly tent in Yonkers with its moldy history books to go back to.

I clenched my fists.

They'd stolen themselves away from me a long time ago. So why did this hurt so badly?

I clenched my jaw.

"Our tentacled rulers want good PR," I said softly. They needed the fight to fade away. They needed to hobble the protestors. They needed to kneecap the leaders of the movement.

They needed to kneecap my parents.

Death was one way. "There's another," I said.

"Huh?" Stafford asked.

"There's another way they can neutralize my parents," I said. I knew what it was. That anger I'd been building inside had steered me toward a solution, and now it faded to sadness.

Stafford looked curious. "What do you mean?"

"Me," I said. "You can use me."

Stafford leaned back, then cleared all the documents off the table with a wave of his hand. "I'm listening."

"If I do this, I want to see them. I want to see them today," I said. Because in order to save my family, I would have to first destroy it.

"I can arrange something," Stafford said.

I took a deep breath and paused. Could I do what I was planning?

Yes. To save their lives. I could do this.

I had to. Angry as I might be, what sort of son would I be if I watched them die and didn't try to stop it?

The electrified fence between us prevented any touching. My dad stood in the middle of his cell, avoiding the walls like I had. But he'd spent all day in the sun, and the bags under his eyes from lack of sleep, food, and drink made him look older and frail. His salt-and-pepper hair hung every which way.

He licked bloodied, sun-cracked lips, and hung his head when he saw me enter.

My mother, in the other cell, had managed to fold her legs into a tight cradle so she could sit down, but she also looked frazzled and exhausted. Her normally even brown skin was splotchy with dirt and streaked with blood from a cut on her scalp. Dried blood also stained her shoulders.

"Oh God. Dev!" She tried to stand, but shrank back into her position when the cell sparked. Mine had just been hot, theirs was designed for maximum misery. "You're alive."

"Mom." I put a finger carefully between the spaces in the metal grid so we could touch fingertips gently. "I'm okay."

"I'm so sorry, Dev. We can't even get to talk to Stephan. I'm so sorry. It's very bad. All those Accordance soldiers in armor, they didn't care. They shot people. Right in the street. Live, on camera."

She was shaking. In shock. It must be a war zone on 110th Street, I realized. Other prisoners in the cages looked worse than my parents. Blood-splattered clothes, distant stares.

Gunshot wounds, jagged wounds. Ignored, without medics, some of the protestors trapped out here would die.

"Mom, you know I love you," I said tentatively.

"Of course. They said there was a chance you might . . . not be in the same position we are." Her brown eyes teared up. She whispered now, not wanting my father to listen in. "You have to take that. And don't feel guilty about it. Anything we've done, it's only hurt you. And I'm sorry about that. What we've done, it's us. Okay? It's us. You run, like I told you. You run from all this."

I closed my eyes. "I know." My voice cracked.

"Devlin?" My dad had cocked his head to stare at me. He used his teacher voice, strong and commanding attention even in his state. "What's going on?"

"I can save you." I took a deep breath filled with the smell of blood, unwashed bodies, and sewage. "But I'm going to have to say . . . some things. I'm going to have to do things." I closed my eyes, focusing on the unsteady pressure of my mom's fingertip against mine. A single line of contact. All I would have.

Sometimes I thought about why family members always fought so hard with each other; maybe it was because they were the only ones who could get fully into each other's heads. Dad saw through me instantly. "Don't do what you're thinking," he said. "That's everything we've been fighting against. We're trying to stop you from having to fight their wars for them. You know none of the recruits they've taken off-Earth have come back yet. We're trying to build a different future for you."

"Well, that didn't work too well, did it, Dad?" I snapped. "So what other choice do I have?"

"You have choices. You *always* have choices," he said.

17

"Like letting you die? What the hell kind of human being would I be if I let my own parents be executed?" I shouted, my voice quavering. Hold it together, I told myself. I bit my lip and calmed down. "There is no choice. The only choice is what you do with the second chance I'm buying you. Maybe you both try to sneak more antioccupation activity in, and I come back and find you dead anyway. Or maybe you get jobs, keep your heads down, and I live to come back and see you again."

Or maybe, I thought into the silence, we all would die for nothing. I opened my burning eyes to look at my angry, confused, hurt parents. Just as I knew they would be.

You're welcome, Stafford, I thought. I'm breaking them. I'm taking it all out from under them. And in some ways, they would consider it worse than death.

"You sign up to fight for the Accordance," my mom said, "then they've trapped you. They've talked you into this. Don't do what they tell you. Don't *collaborate*."

That word. I pulled my finger back. "I'm sorry."

A struthiform guard opened the gate leading out. Stafford waited for me on the other side. "Time's up," he said, pointedly avoiding looking at any of the prisoners.

"You'll be under house arrest," I told my parents. "You'll get filmed going there. But it will be safe. And good." And it would make them look utterly like they had made a deal, and would undercut their authority in the eyes of the antioccupation movement.

My dad grabbed the wire mesh. Sparks danced around his fists. He was crying, out of pain from the electrified wire or from my betrayal. I didn't know which. "You don't let them change you, Devlin. You find ways to fight them. In your own way. Like I raised you. You stay *human*!"

3

A human policeman in yellow uniform opened the van door with a crunchy squeak. I looked out warily. Leftovers from the protest filled 110th Street. The ripped pieces of the command tents blew up against stacked metal barricades, along with the detritus of protestors who'd fled.

Or been dragged away.

"You've got two hundred feet to walk on your own." Stafford directed me forward. "We'll be watching you."

The door slammed shut behind me. For the first time in twenty-four hours, sunshine hit my face and free air blew past me. I was free. Free for the two hundred feet between me and the gates of the Accordance Administrative Complex.

I picked my way around the trash and the barricades.

Halfway to the great legs of the administration buildings, I wondered if I could still run.

No. My parents were still in Accordance hands. Running would do nothing. I wasn't really free. These two hundred feet I walked on my own were as much a cage as the heated cage I'd been penned in.

Other volunteers straggled down the street toward the two-story skeletal gates that locked down the forest of the Accordance Administrative Complex against the world around it. Four or five of the volunteers rubbed their wrists, now free of their shackles. "Volunteers." They'd spent time in the fenced cells as well.

I wondered what horrible choices they'd had to make.

A drone buzzed overhead and blasted hot air into my face. We were live for the world to watch. Earth volunteers, signing up to join the Accordance's war against the Conglomeration. Rise, you sons and daughters of Earth, to help the Accordance defend a vulnerable world.

"Look at them," one of my fellow travelers said, acid in her voice. She nodded her head across the street. Ten well-dressed volunteers ambled down from the Harlem gates, where their parents clustered near struthiform guards, waving.

The volunteers waved back at their families, then at the drones in the air.

"I want to punch the shit-eating grins off their entitled faces," the girl next to me muttered. "Our future officer class. My dad says Harlem used to be all human-held. He grew up there. After it was all evacuated and the buildings seized, it became just collaborators and aliens. You look familiar; do I know you?"

"No," I said. Then, "I don't know."

"Keep moving!" Human soldiers in gray uniforms with no sign of rank on their shoulders waited on the other side of the black, bony gates. They herded us into lines that snaked through three booths in the middle of the glassy road, shoving us until we stood where they wanted.

Struthiform officers in red armor with oversize eyes and bobbing heads trotted up and down our lines, their necks undulating this way and that. "Walk through the scanners, hold your breath. Do not move," they ordered.

"Where are the scanners?" I asked.

A feathered arm shoved me forward until I stood on a blue circle in the road between two booths.

A blast of air hit my groin. I gasped. As I crouched and swore, a spinning tube of glass shot up out of the ground around me, then dropped right back down. A struthiform technician in the booth on my right glanced briefly at a three-dimensional skeleton that appeared in the air between him and me. My skeleton. Visible to everyone in line. Then it turned into an image of my skeleton with internal organs. Then my skin filled in. I was naked in front of everyone behind me in line until the technician waved the image away.

"Move!" he ordered.

My embarrassment hadn't even had time to form when the struthiform behind me shoved me forward so that the next recruit could stand in my place.

"Run! Run!" Pushed forward by other recruits and struthiforms yelling at us, we jogged under the shadowed roads and around the great twisted legs of the lower buildings.

A hundred of us stopped as one on a patch of grass. A plaza in the heart of the alien forest of a city buried in the heart of New York. A human sergeant in gray marched up to our front.

I'd seen his type before: on commercial breaks between sports, on public service announcements on screens in delis.

"Listen up, you useless maggots," he shouted, amplified words ringing out throughout the plaza. "There are many aliens out there. They come in all sorts of shapes and sizes. . . ."

Fuck. This was really happening.

I was going to become one of those people who disap-peared off into deep Accordance space and had yet to come back.

Sweat trickled down the small of my back as I focused on an orb-shaped drone flying around the crowd for close-ups. I half listened to the description of our five enemies and what they could do to us.

I was going to let myself get shot across space. I was going to leave Earth far, far behind, and go fight a war that would be light-years away. With creatures that I'd never seen with my own eyes.

And I was going to do it for another bunch of alien creatures.

The human sergeant finished his well-rehearsed speech and left. The cameras flew away. Struthiforms yelled at us again. A line formed.

"Hold out your forearm." The man in front of me held what looked like a nail gun.

I did, and then winced as it punctured my skin with a sharp pneumatic hiss. I looked down. A single bead of blood welled up in the center of a tattoo of a stylized Earth with a triangle in the middle. My skin sizzled around it for a second.

"What's this?"

"Your rank and ID. Welcome to the Colonial Protection Forces. Move along."

I stumbled forward. Another annoying orb camera dropped out of the air to eye level and circled around me as a man stepped forward. "Mr. Hart, I'm Vincent Anais, with Colonial Broadcast Agency. If it's okay with you, I'd like to have a moment." His voice indicated he wasn't asking a question. I noticed he had a CPF tattoo on his forearm as well. His had two dots underneath the triangle.

"Um . . ."

"Just relax, smile, and one, two, three. . . . Mr. Hart, what prompted you to volunteer to join the fight against the Conglomeration?"

I licked my lips and tried not to look at the drone and its spiderlike clusters of unblinking camera lenses. "I . . . just want to do my bit to serve, and protect our world."

"And how did your parents feel about this, Mr. Hart? Are they proud you joined the CPF?"

I gritted my teeth. "I think they understand why it was important that I make this choice."

Anais smiled broadly. "So they weren't happy about it?"

"No," I told him. "No, they were not."

"Thank you for your time, Mr. Hart. And thank you for your service. Your world appreciates it."

The drone flew away, and Anais leaned forward. "Off the record, kid: You're going to have to do a lot better than that if you want your family to stay out of trouble."

Kid? Really? He was calling me a kid? *Who the fuck was he?* "I gave you what you needed," I snapped. "I'm here, aren't I? You got me to join, now leave me the hell alone."

Anais grabbed my collar and yanked me forward. When I tried to pull away from him, he tightened his grip. "Listen," he hissed. "I saw you tuning out the speech the sergeant gave back there. You think it's all just words. But what's out there, it's real. There's a black hole of an alien empire out there, reshaping the galaxy for its own purposes. It is old, implacable, and more alien than the aliens around us. The CPF needs minds and bodies to fight for the Accordance. This isn't about your wounded pride, or your family's. It's about something far, far bigger. Your usefulness as a tool to the CPF is just beginning. So get with the fucking program and start selling it, or it's going to get far worse, recruit."

4

Fifteen recruits, dressed up in their grays, stood with me in the train car as the countryside swept by at five hundred miles an hour on the high-speed rail line from New York to Richmond. The sort of high-speed rail that Americans had never been able to build until the Occupation, as Accordance propaganda was always fond of pointing out. "You are about to meet the acting president of the Regional American Council," Anais said.

He walked back and forth in front of us.

"This is a big fucking deal," Anais said slowly. "President Barnett has been an important part of Colonial Administration for a decade now. You will shake his hand. You will answer his questions. Then you will circulate and shake more hands. Be polite, be enthusiastic. Got it?"

"Yes, sir," we shouted back.

Anais sighed and then practically growled back at us. "How many times do I have to tell you there are no 'sirs' here in the CPF! The Arvani don't want tribal honorifics. Drop that shit. And definitely drop that shit in front of any Accordance. Got it?"

"Yes, s—" We choked back the follow-up word as Anais stared us down.

Once Anais left the train car, we relaxed.

I'd expected boot camp. But yesterday I'd been peeled off from my fellow trainees, stuffed into dress grays, and ordered out into an oval courtyard. A wasp-shaped Accordance ship spiraled down out of the sky, engines kicking up grass as it settled on its skids, and Anais had prodded us aboard.

I paused near the heavy door that swung up, looking over at the bulging engine pods sticking out from either side. Deep inside the engines, dark matter collided and swirled around, as advanced to human nuclear technology as a reactor might be to someone accustomed to shoveling coal into a steam-powered engine.

"What's the matter, recruit?" Anais asked. "Never been flying before?"

"Not in an Accordance jumpship," I said.

"Not a jumpship," Anais said. "Jumpships go to orbit. The engines on this aren't powerful enough, though the frame looks similar. We call these hoppers. Intra-atmosphere only."

The engines kicked the ship off the ground, rattling us around inside as we bumped and shook into the air. A few hundred feet up, the pods rotated, and then a subsonic thump shivered through the hopper as we sped up. A minute later the hopper hit supersonic.

After the flight from New York to London, we'd publicly helped other recruits get tattooed and inducted into the Colonial Protection Forces. And I'd been interviewed again about my parents. Again I'd all but disowned them, and talked about my pride in protecting my world. Only this time, with Anais watching me like a hawk.

At the repurposed barracks of Windsor Castle, we'd jogged

around the courtyards for the cameras, waved, and then boarded another Accordance hopper to Jakarta. And then we'd come back to New York for another recruitment drive. I'd done interviews near the steps of the Empire State Building, which had been converted into a barracks for CPF soldiers.

And now we approached the city of Richmond.

"Don't look so glum," Hammond told me. An older recruit, in his twenties, he came from a predominantly Accordance-owned area of Harlem. "Make them happy, you get an early discharge and a spot in civil service. Get a job in Colonial Administration and you're set for life."

DC's ruins swept by our windows. Swamp crept over the rubble of the city. The white, skeletal remains of several walls and some columns flashed by as the rail line cut through the heart of the demolished capital.

"Colonial Administration is for aliens, you idiot," another recruit said from the bar. She shook her head. "You'll work for them, but you're not going to advance up the political chain."

"Sounds about right," I said.

"What the hell do you think you know? They're not going to hand you a position: Your parents are terrorists," Hammond snapped. "In fact, be careful. You screw this up for us, I'll fuck you up so hard you won't even remember your own name. Only reason you're here is to shit on your parents."

I took a deep breath. I wanted to jump across the velvety carpet and punch him in the face.

But if I blew this opportunity, my parents would suffer.

Hammond saw the resignation on my face and laughed. "Thought so."

I stalked out of the train car to try to get some space to myself to stew. I wandered out to look at the other inhabitants headed for Richmond. The rich and powerful, the humans who worked with their alien rulers to help keep everything down here running nice and smoothly. They sipped champagne and chatted about stock prices; their eyes widened when they saw my uniform.

I wasn't on duty. I didn't have to suffer their inane questions and chatter, so I just kept walking. I stopped when I reached the locked doors leading to the alien section of the train.

No humans past this point.

I turned around and walked back.

Acting president Barnett took over the capitol building in Richmond as his private estate when he ascended to power in the Colonial Administration. Through the heavily guarded gates, we could see the tall white building within Accordance-built walls that defended the complex.

Between us and the walls: hundreds of protestors. Not nearly as thick a crowd as New York, but still determined.

"Jesus, you'd think they'd have learned by now," Hammond said.

"Okay recruits," Anais shouted. "You're in after our guests get rolling. Shoulders back, beam with pride, and let's get inside."

"What about the protestors?" I asked. They didn't look disciplined. And they weren't standing in any authorized zone.

Anais looked blankly at me. "What about them?"

Hammond shoved me forward and hissed, "Grow a pair."

We staggered forward. The upper-crust guests roared ahead in armored vehicles, struthiform soldiers running alongside them. Unlike the armor on the soldiers in New York, this black-and-red armor covered the aliens entirely. They ran easily, joints making a loud snicking sound. Powered armor,

I realized. The struthiforms were as protected as the vehicles, and far more dangerous.

It didn't take more than a few seconds for the fifteen of us to fall in line and walk. Our routine fell into place easily, even after just a few days of practice: Wave for camera drones. Look like excited recruits.

Inside there would be good food. All we had to do was shake politicians' hands. Pose next to the human machine that kept Accordance interests on Earth running smoothly.

And all I had to do was try not to think of my parents seeing the images.

"This isn't like the other protests," someone said, eyeing the crowds shouting at us. Usually we heard words like "traitor" or "collaborator." Since the occupation, and then Pacification, most countries had been following the same pattern as the one in the Americas: peaceful protest. Carefully organized, very publicized.

The Pacification came after the occupation, when humanity rose up to fight on the streets and the Accordance responded. At the time I was only five, but I'd watched the grainy, green nighttime livestreams of hunks of rock arcing across the sky to descend on Jeddah, Moscow, and Cleveland. The plumes of debris that kept rising and rising into the air, all that was left of the cities.

The Accordance did not like dissent.

This crowd had worked itself up to spittle-flecking anger.

"Are those flags?" Hammond asked, in shock. "They're illegal."

I recognized the X pattern of stars and stripes. "It used to be the flag for the South," I told him.

"Like Old Mexico?" he asked.

He didn't recognize the flag. No one taught indigenous

history anymore. Accordance-approved history downplayed smaller regional history for a big sweep. Indigenous history is not conducive to their desire to create a global human culture and to reduce regionalism.

That was how my father had lost his job at NYU. Teaching US history in too much detail. Not enough focus on the UN and larger regional commonalities, as the Accordance ordered.

"It's nationalistic," Hammond muttered, disgust in his voice.

My father's lecturing voice bubbled to the tip of my tongue as I prepared to educate Hammond. But a bottle of liquid struck the ground in front of us and exploded.

"Molotov cocktail!" someone shouted. Fire spread across the road, separating the line of recruits.

Ahead of us, on the other side of the fire, I saw Anais look back. He spoke into his wrist, annoyed. One of the recruits swore up a storm as he kicked and stamped out his smoldering pants.

The struthiform soldiers snapped back around in unison, flocking together as they loped through the guttering fire left by the bottle's debris. They broke free of their tight cluster a second later as another bottle arced up over the crowd at them.

The foremost struthiform leapt twenty feet into the air, following the arc of the homemade explosive, and scattered protestors when it landed in their midst. A man struck the alien on the back with a tire iron, and the struthiform back-handed him.

I watched the man fly through the air, arms flailing until he hit the wall with a wet sound. He slumped to the ground and didn't move.

"Get over here," Anais shouted. I realized it was the second or third time he'd yelled at us: We'd just frozen in place.

Several gunmen mixed in with the crowd opened fire on

the struthiforms. Bullets thwacked against alien armor over the crackle of little fires left from the Molotov cocktails.

Not all the protestors had been planning violence. Most of them scattered. I fixed on one mother and her son, who looked about eight years old, as they ran past. Her head snapped back and misted red blood in the air around us, then she pitched to the ground.

The kid fell with her, eyes wide and screaming. He scrabbled in the dirty road and picked up a rock.

I ran. Not even thinking twice.

He threw the rock past me at the nearest Accordance soldier. When it struck armor, the struthiform spun and aimed. Shielding the kid behind me, I held my hands up and winced, closing my eyes.

The shot never came.

Anais grabbed my hair and yanked me out of my half crouch. "Move!" he screamed. Struthiform soldiers fell in on either side of us.

Everyone retreated through the gates, which snapped shut after us with startling speed.

"What the hell were you thinking?" Anais shouted at me. "What the fucking hell were you thinking?"

"Sir . . ."

I bit my tongue and let the last part of the word hang in the air as Anais glared at me. "You stood down an Accordance soldier. You're lucky it didn't just shoot you."

"It was going to shoot a child," I said.

"You should have stood aside and let it do what it needed to do," Anais said. He grabbed my elbow hard, the points of his fingers digging into the flesh to bruise muscle as he shoved me up the great steps into the capitol building. Two human guards in light armor stood on either side of the columns.

"Inside," Anais snapped.

One of the recruits sat on the ground, blood covering her grays. A medic squatted next to her, sealing a wound with a spray can of bioglue and checking vitals.

We were in a foyer. I could see that beyond the doors a reception under crystal chandeliers was quietly going on. Men in suits, struthiforms with red command strips located just above their wings on their tailored uniforms. A carapoid lumbered around a corner of the room, moving a large table full of drinks into place.

And I noticed something that made my mouth go dry. A spherical tank of clear water wrapped around the bullet-shaped flesh of what looked like an octopus, but most certainly wasn't.

Arvani. The tentacles under the clear, body-conforming tank were mechanized, wrapped around the Arvani's natural tentacles. They undulated, shifting the tank expertly around as the alien rose up on the tips of its tentacles to look at a human politician eye to eye.

The creators and leaders of the Accordance.

Only a handful of Arvani lived down on the surface. They preferred their space stations, filled with giant pools that let them re-create their oceanic home environs. When they did live on the surface, they preferred the coasts.

A politician ignored the whole reception to stride through the doors toward us. He carried a bottle in one hand, a glass in another. Acting president Barnett, seventy years old, scowled as his pinched, leathery face regarded the scene in his foyer.

Anais left to talk to someone by a marble pedestal. Barnett focused on me. "I just looked over the video. You're the idiot who stood in front of the kid?"

My mouth dry, I nodded.

Barnett motioned me closer. He rubbed absentmindedly at a dry, bloodshot eye. "I have five women waiting for me back in my bedroom. Can you imagine that? A whole damn harem. They're buck naked and standing along the side of the mirrored wall for me. You know how many pills I have to take just to keep up with that? You can't imagine. Maybe you can, you're young. I'll bet you can imagine all sorts of things. Multiply it, son. I've done things that would've shocked even me when I was your age."

This was not what I expected. I also didn't want to think about the president naked and sweaty . . . No. Just no. What the hell was happening?

"You know," Barnett said. "I used to hate people like you."

"Younger . . . ?" I floundered. I saw this man on screens all the time. Yet here he stood in front of me, swaying slightly.

"Brown," Barnett said bluntly. He poured some of the amber alcohol into the glass in his other hand. He drank it like someone thirsty would down a glass of water. "Brown people."

I didn't know what to say to that. I stood and blinked.

"You look tan. Hard to tell. Maybe you're out in the sun too much. Maybe you have a background. Where's your mother from?" Barnett moved closer to me. The smell of alcohol rolled out of his pores. I was surprised his clothes weren't dripping with it.

I didn't want to answer. But this was the acting president of the Americas, and I could recognize the ton of shit I'd stepped into. "Puerto Rico," I stammered.

He nodded knowingly. "Thought so. Latina. Nice. . . . During the occupation, I linked up with my fellow soldiers in units all over the South. We negotiated with the Accordance to stand down. It was the Federal's fight with the ETs, not ours. We saw a chance to rise again, we took it. Now, from Richmond to Tampa, ain't nothing but the right kind of churches, and the right kind of folk. And you know what?"

I shook my head. I didn't.

"We all still have problems. The poverty, that didn't go away. Those people out there, they're still facing seeing their children get drafted. Or 'volunteered.' That's why they're angry. Angry because they can't eat. Because they barely have any work to go around, unless it's for the Accordance. Angry because there's still some war off in the distance. And they're angry at me. I thought it would get better. I was wrong. And now, I know things. The Accordance: They've shown me what's coming. And I'm going to eat, screw, and party until I drop dead. I'd recommend you try the same."

Anais smoothly appeared next to us both. "Mr. President, your presence is needed."

Barnett glanced over at the two Arvani in their mechanized water tanks waiting for him. "Well, fuck. Here we go. Time to be obsequious and do my duty."

Anais held up an open palm with a pair of blue pills in it. "Your personal aide suggested I pass these on."

"Ah." Barnett picked up one of them and eyed it. "You're going to make me sober up. Do you know how much expensive bourbon it took for me to get to where I am right now? Never mind, rhetorical question."

He swallowed the pills dry, blinked, and took a deep breath.

Anais indicated that Barnett should go first, but the president grabbed his shoulder. "The Arvani are going to lecture me. Before I go, Anais, make sure this boy is taken care of. If the Accordance bayoneted a kid out there, that mob outside would have overrun my estate."

"The capitol building, you mean?" Anais prompted.

Barnett waved his hand. "Capitol, estate, personal palace. President, ruler, puppet. My head on a pike: We'll see it happen at some point when they get over the walls. I just would rather have some more fun while there's still some life in me yet without some goddamned Accordance soldier screwing me over early. Struthiforms can't tell the difference between a child and a fully grown human because the walking drumsticks lay eggs and leave them, so they don't even understand what a child is. See, that's the problem with aliens on the ground. They're alien. Which I keep saying. But who the fuck listens to me? I'm just the acting president."

Anais glanced at me. "He can't be in the publicity program. There have to be consequences for what he did."

"Let the CPF give him a chance to prove himself. He stood between a soldier in full armor and a kid. Do your president a solid: Send him to the Hamptons instead of . . . what you're planning."

I looked at them both, but they avoided my eyes.

Anais finally sighed. "Okay, Mr. President. The Hamptons it is."

5

The hopper rattled and shook as it flew us over the American East Coast. I sat on a plain bench with Anais on one side of me, and on the other side an unshaven, older Colonial Protection Forces soldier who looked supremely bored.

I twisted my wrists. The zip ties cut into my skin, but neither of them had cared about my complaints. Right now, I was still technically a prisoner. A recruit who'd gotten in the way of the Accordance military doing their job.

The soldier propped up two prosthetic legs against the bench on the other side, leaned back with crossed arms, and closed his eyes.

"Anais, what about my parents?" I asked.

"What about them?"

"Are they going to be executed, now that everything is changing? What's going to happen?" I was scared that a split-second decision was going to ruin it all. All the sacrifices I'd made. "Anais, please help. If everything I've done is for nothing—"

"Help? Help?" Anais groaned. "I've done nothing but help

you and you've blown it. Who *helped* coach you to sell your story better? Who shepherded you kids around the world? Who ran into the fucking fire to drag your ass out to safety? I did. I did that. Now you're whining about more help. You know what you haven't done? Have you thanked me? Once? Have you ever thought about the fact that all of this isn't just about you?"

I pulled back from his anger. "It's your job," I protested.

"My job is to take willing recruits and parade them around the world for PR purposes. If I really gave a shit about nothing but my job, I'd only take recruits from families that worked closely with the Accordance. I wouldn't have helped you save your parents' lives by letting you into the program. To be honest, I may not be making that mistake again."

I resisted Anais's words. I couldn't find it in my heart to give him credit for doing the good thing. It was the minimum.

And yet. He was right. He could make things simpler. And he hadn't. And that said . . . something.

"As for your parents," Anais said, "I don't see the point in sending a recruit to training knowing his parents are about to die. That shit isn't going to make a good soldier. No, the deal stands. The deal stands because you were on live TV, standing in front of a child. You risked your life to protect, and we're spinning that. You're about to get the promotion that you've been begging for, because you want to protect more than just a child in a riot."

"A promotion?" I was zip-tied and locked to a bench in an Accordance vehicle. There were no portholes, just turbulence and whining motors. I didn't feel like I was getting a promotion.

"Promotion to combat. Real action."

The old soldier on my other side spoke up. "Congratulations, boot. You're about to become cannon fodder. You could have spent your whole enlistment being an actor in uniform. Simple exercises, safe on Earth. Now, no more TV appearances. No champagne with politicians. No handshakes. No jogging along nice boulevards with security."

Anais smiled sadly. "He's right."

The hopper pitched up and shook, the engines whined as we suddenly dumped velocity. The CPF soldier staggered up and slid the side door open with a grunt.

"Your home for the next couple days," he shouted back over the wind.

We glided through the air over the Hamptons. Obstacles littered the beach. The remains of bombed-out mansions used for target practice slumped over into sandy grasses. Bunkers pocked the landscape like inside-out barnacles, hoppers lined up on landing pads around them. Barracks clustered around bulldozed pits, and I saw several squads of humans running in formation.

The hopper slid over it all and dropped the last hundred feet down to the beach, kicking up a maelstrom of sand and water.

Anais cut the zip ties loose and pointed at the door. "If you make it back, look me up," he said, not unkindly. "I'll buy you your first drink."

The soldier grabbed my collar. "Welcome to the first day of the rest of your war," he shouted into my ear.

Then he threw me out of the hopper and into the storm.

I choked and tried to cover my face as wet sand blasted my exposed skin. The hopper eased back into the sky, and the flurry stilled. I wiped caked sand away from my face and stood up.

Four other hoppers slapped down onto the beach. Three or four recruits tumbled out the doors of each hopper, landing awkwardly in the sand and staggering in the blast of air as the vehicles rose back into the sky.

We milled around, pulling closer together as we watched the insectile aircraft skim out over the ocean, then bank south together in formation.

"Anyone know where we're supposed to go next?" a girl nervously asked. She hugged herself, and her wide-eyed fear created a sort of boundary around her. Everyone stepped back, as if worried they might catch it.

We glanced up at the sound of a loud buzz. A carapoid, wings fully extended, finished a ten-foot jump over our heads and landed in the sand near the water.

We all gaped. No one had ever seen one of the beetle-like aliens in armor. It looked like a mobile tank with scuttling feet as it moved toward us, holding a raised baton in one of its knobby hands.

It jammed the stick into a puddle of salt water. The stick sizzled and spat, and the puddle of water exploded from the jolt cast by the mother of all cattle prods.

We all reflexively jumped back. "Jesus," someone muttered. "Is that our drill instructor?"

"What are any of you good for?" the carapoid asked in a hiss augmented by the heavy segments of gray armor molded to its mandibles. They creaked as it moved. "Do you have any survival instincts? Or will you be the first to die when it gets really ugly? Do you have any talents to offer me? Because right now you all seem bewildered and scared, and that's not what I need. But maybe I have trouble interpreting your ugly alien faces and you're all ready to go. Either way, you are here so that we learn where best you might serve."

The carapoid moved over the sand, thudding its way around the group, eyeing us through compound eyes protected by scarred blast-proof goggles backlit with heads-up display information.

It tapped the prod against the armored carapace. Tick, tick, tick.

None of us said anything.

"The Accordance sacrifices much to keep an umbrella over your heads, and you're all cowering on this beach like hatchlings on a mother's stomach," the carapoid said. "So let's shake you loose and see whether you can scuttle on your own, yes?"

We all looked at each other.

Tick. Tick. Tick. "See that pier out there? I'm going to start walking toward it after you. Anyone I catch up with, I'm going to tap to encourage them. Ready? Go."

For a second we all remained frozen. Then the carapoid reached out with the prod and gently tapped the nearest recruit. The tip sizzled and snapped, and electricity danced across his shoulder.

He screamed and leapt into motion, staggering away from the carapoid drill instructor. I needed no similar convincing. I ran.

I'd been on a hunger strike the last week. This week I'd been drinking punch and flying around the world to parade myself as a new recruit. I was jet-lagged and bewildered. Out of breath.

Smaller, faster recruits than me ran past as I struggled to keep to the middle of the pack, highly aware that just a few people struggled on behind me in the wet sand.

Zap! I glanced behind to see the girl with wide eyes eat sand as the carapoid got within reach and tapped her.

She lay facedown on the beach, quivering, as several of the other girls gave her and the drill instructor a wide berth to pelt for the pier. They passed me by; I'd slowed down as I'd looked behind.

I snapped my attention forward and ran like hell, passing a purple-haired girl wearing a leather jacket and jeans. She glanced over at me, and her eyes glinted silver in the sunlight. A couple years older than me, than most of the recruits, she looked pissed, not scared like the rest of us.

We all made it to the piers. I grabbed one of the weathered pylons and panted, holding myself up.

"This won't do," the alien drill instructor said as it trundled up to the heaving, exhausted mess of us scattered around the pylons. It moved around on its many legs to face back down the beach, then turned back to us. "Again!"

It squeezed the prod. Sparks ran threateningly up and down it.

The group took off. But the girl with the silver eyes walked up to the carapoid. "This is stupid," she said calmly.

I stayed to watch, still catching my breath, ready to run like hell.

"What?"

"You've figured out who can run faster," she said. "But what the fuck does that have to do with who can fight the best? Unless you're planning on putting us into battles where we run away from the enemy a lot."

The carapoid rubbed its forehands together, making a cricket-like chirp. "Now, there's some spit," it said. "Well done. You're right. This exercise tells us nothing about you other than who can run the fastest, and that's not all we're looking for. There will be more tests, don't you worry about that. But what it also tells us is—"

It slammed her on the chest with the prod. She fell back against the pylon behind her, but surprisingly kept standing.

From her jacket rose a wisp of smoke, and she quickly shucked it off and let it drop to the sand by her feet.

"It also tells us who follows orders! Now follow my damn orders and run!"

We both took off down the beach.

A boy with thick shoulders stood on a chair in the center of the mess hall. His skin dripped salt water from his grays, and he'd shaved his head down to the scalp to reveal a custom CPF Earth-and-triangle tattoo on the back of his neck.

For the whole day we'd been run back and forth down the beach. Until recruits dropped to the sand and wouldn't move. Until we coughed, our lungs burned, and our muscles gave out.

Human medics checked over recruits with burn marks on their skin as we milled about and eyed the kitchen's empty counters. The food that had been left out had been snapped up by the runners who got to the mess hall first.

Runners like the kid with the South African accent standing on the chair.

"Today, you learned something about yourselves," he shouted at us. "About the warriors you really are. Or aren't. Over the next few days, we will find out who the true fighters are, and who will be our support staff mopping the barracks while we fight to protect Earth!"

"Sounds like a lot of bullshit," I muttered.

Someone next to me snorted. I hadn't realized I'd said that out loud. I was more tired than I realized. She nodded though. "His name's Ken Awojobi. He was on my transport in. His family is in deep with the Accordance. He's on the officer track, and he knows it. Been training and studying for this his whole life. A chance to serve, gain rank, then come out high for something in Accordance civil service. Maybe run a partition, or something nice like that."

I wasn't too tired to smile and hold a hand out. "I'm Devlin," I said.

"Cee Cee." Cee Cee was a head shorter than me. She'd pulled her blond hair back in a tight ponytail. The corners of her eyes fluoresced with processor ink tattoos. Extra augmentation.

"What is he doing?" I asked out loud.

Ken had pulled out a pair of clippers. "You, grab him."

A nearby recruit squirmed and kicked at the two lean recruits pinning him down. Ken grabbed his head and the clippers bit down.

"This is crazy," I said, looking around for the drill instructor.

"It's all a test," Cee Cee said. "Look." I followed her eyes to the upper corners of the room.

"What?"

"Cameras. I can sense their link-ups." She tapped the nano-ink beside her eyes. "They're watching us. All the time. We're being studied. Smile."

"Just keep moving and keep people between us and the idiot with the clippers," I muttered, and tried to put a hand on her lower back. A bit of showmanship that I couldn't help.

But my plan didn't work. Ken spotted the movement. He swaggered over and flipped the clippers on and off. "Worried about losing a little hair? Think it'll mess with your good looks?" He glanced at Cee Cee and smiled.

"Look," I said. "They have official barbers; if we're going to get shaved down, they'll do it." Ken didn't need to parade around as if he were in charge. Although, from what Cee Cee said, he probably would end up being in charge anyway.

"Oh, but this is *tradition*," Ken said.

"I don't care," I said. Why was I bristling so much? "It's not your place."

Ken's eyes flashed. "Not my place?"

"Look—" As I said that, Ken grabbed my head with one hand. "Hey!"

"I know who you are, asshole," he hissed. I jerked back from him, the clippers snarling and catching my neck. Hair fell down between us as I twisted away. Two of Ken's "assistants" grabbed my arms. I tried to yank free, but they were strong, their fingers bruising me as they shoved me down onto a table. "Seen you on TV. Seen your parents. You're traitors, anti-Accordance. So you might fool some people, by pretending to join. But anyone who looks closely can see you don't give a shit about all this. You're half-assing it."

Metal ran up my scalp and more hair flurried around me and landed on the table shoved against my face.

"Fuck you." I squirmed and tried to kick backward. I got a knee, and a curse.

"There's some real, actual fight in him," Ken announced to the room. "He's not as much of a pacifist coward as his parents after all." He dug an elbow into the back of my neck and I gasped. The clippers nicked my left ear, and I felt a little trickle of blood run down the lobe.

Ken shoved himself away from me, and I jumped up, my face hot with humiliation. Fists balled, I growled, but he just laughed and stepped away as his newfound groupies made a wall in front of him and shook their heads.

Five recruits now surrounded him like bodyguards.

Six on one. Two of them older, large biceps under their gray T-shirts.

I was going to get my ass handed to me. And Ken knew it. He smiled, daring me to try. Everyone else had seen the logic of not trying it.

Fast. I'd have to get past them and focus on getting just one punch in. One punch to show the room that Ken wasn't invincible. To make a point.

To prove that I wasn't a coward to everyone watching.

"Lights out in two minutes!" a human drill instructor shouted from across the room. "Anyone not in an assigned bunk will spend the night on the beach with me. Your names are on your bunks. Go!"

The larger threat scattered us.

I jogged through the hallway, looking for the bunks, exhausted, hungry, still tense with anger. I stopped when I saw a water fountain.

"We don't have time for that," someone passing me hissed.

I kept drinking water. Until I felt like something in my stomach was going to burst. Part of me was trying to fill that hole the hunger had excavated in me. But I also had another trick up my sleeve.

The end of the corridor opened up into an almost warehouse-sized room. Hundreds of bunk beds in rows in the open area. To the back, bathrooms and showers.

I jumped into my lower bunk. Looked around. "Hey, upstairs," I asked the bunk above me. "Is it all boys in one row and girls in the next?"

"As far as I can see," the voice replied tiredly.

"Huh."

"I wouldn't get out of the bed at night, though." The bed shifted, and a brown face peered over at me. Curved gang sigils marked the massive forearm dangling over the side.

"Why not?"

"Force fields. I got here a day early. Our overlords aren't interested in anyone here getting into trouble at night. We might as well be in a jail cell come lights-out."

And just as he said it, the lights cut out.

There was some muttering chatter between the rows— invitations—and then a sound like a bug getting zapped in one of those bug lights. Someone screamed and swore.

"See?" Upstairs laughed.

"Shit. When do they turn back off?"

"Hoping to make friends with someone you met?"

"No, I drank a lot of water. I'm going to have to pee," I told him. "I wanted to wake up early, but now I'm wondering how I take a piss in the middle of the night."

My bunkmate's face came back over the edge. "Up early," he said thoughtfully. "That's smart. What's your name again? I saw it when I got to the bunk, but forgot."

"Devlin," I said.

"Rakwon." Rakwon extended his hand over the edge of the bed. I shook it. It was a big, strong hand. I felt like a child.

"You play sports?" I asked.

"No. Everyone asks. We run big in my family. I guess it's because my mother's Samoan. Dad's from Queens. My brother played rugby, but quit after he lost a tooth." He laughed. "If you don't piss the bed tonight, wake me up with you. The fields turn off right before breakfast. Getting there first while everyone is getting their bearings is a good idea."

Another loud zap, this time swearing in a decidedly female timbre.

"The fields are up across beds as well. So it's only bunk-mates that can move around. Get some sleep, don't pee yourself. Wake me up when you get up."

We converged on breakfast like a barbarian horde, up before the force fields around our bunks dropped out, waiting for the telltale shimmer in the air to fade away.

The line cooks ladled porridge-like goop into divots in our trays. At the end of the counters were squares of what looked like unwrapped energy bars near large baskets of fist-sized gray blobs.

"What is this shit?" I asked.

Rakwon pointed with a spoon at the goop. "Slurry. Made in Accordance vats and perfectly balanced with all the nutrients a human digestive system needs. You can live off it forever."

"And this?" I shoved the gray blob. It wobbled.

"Energy drink, kinda. Sharpens focus. And hydrates. You can eat the film that holds it together." Rakwon bit into his blob and slurped hard to get the liquid out before it dribbled out from the collapsing spheroid. Then, like slurping spaghetti, he sucked the remains in and chewed them.

"It looks like snot."

Rakwon grinned. "Keep the energy bar in your pocket for later," he said, sliding his square into a pocket of his grays. I did the same.

The slurry tasted vaguely like oatmeal . . . if I used my imagination. I spilled most of the lightly coconut-flavored orb juice down my chin. And I didn't care. We'd got in first, got our table, and had food.

"Holy shit," Cee Cee said. I looked up, mouth full of food, to see the girl with silver eyes and purple ponytail pass us by.

"She tried to stand down the instructor on the beach," I said.

"Those eyes." Cee Cee shook her head. "They would've had to tattoo in the nano-ink with a gun right to the open eyeball."

Rakwon stopped eating and put down his plastic fork. I swallowed; my appetite fled as I thought about a needle striking an eyeball.

"No sedation." Cee Cee winced.

The girl wore her grays now. No street gear. No piercings. But she'd somehow not had her hair shaved down. The purple stood out as she walked between the tables. I noticed processor tats ran down her biceps and forearms in galaxy-like swirls and swoops.

"Hey, hey you!" a smiling boy shouted. "Where *you* from?"

She stopped. He stood in her way. They were face-to-face, food tray to food tray. "Bronx," she said.

"Nah, I mean, where are you *from* from?"

"Castle Hill," she said, looking quite unimpressed.

The boy shook his head. "No, no. Like, where are your *parents* from?"

"Wisconsin and Jersey," she said.

"No, no, you know what I mean."

The girl could have blended into a crowd in some South Asian country. She shoved her interrogator and walked around him with a "Get out of my way." Rakwon laughed. "Bronx," he said.

"Better question is, what's her name," Cee Cee murmured. "She's a walking supercomputer with attitude."

The boy didn't get out of her way, though. He moved back to stand in front of her. "You ain't too polite; I'm just asking you a question," he insisted.

She shoved him again with the flat of her hand. He dropped his tray and pushed her right back. Hard enough she flew back and sprawled hard on the ground.

Everyone froze.

Except for the purple-haired girl. She grabbed a nearby chair and kicked a leg out from it. The metal screws broke right off with the impact.

Then she hit him across the side of the face, using the chair leg like a bat.

He dropped to the ground. She kicked him in the ribs twice, then once in the face. She tossed the leg aside and stepped back, hands in the air, as two human drill instructors ran across the room at them. "He needs help," she called out to them. "He fell into that chair really hard."

They tackled her and dragged her away.

"Washed out in one day," someone said in an awed voice.

There was only cold satisfaction on her face, though. Like she was done playing a silly game she hadn't wanted in on to begin with.

"Glad I didn't say good morning to that one," Rakwon muttered.

"She seemed cute and cuddly to me," I said, still staring at the door she'd been dragged out through.

"A real teddy bear," Cee Cee said. "I'm sure you wouldn't mind trying to put an arm around *her* at night."

"I have a feeling it'd be like hugging a porcupine," Rakwon said.

"Move out!" a carapoid drill instructor shouted from the doors. *"Move out!"*

+ + + +

The drill instructor the previous day hadn't lied. We weren't just running up and down the beach. Now we were tested in other areas. In a room with screens mounted on clear plastic stands, I stared at a holographic display of random parts floating in the air.

"This is a puzzle," said the carapoid alien instructor. "You will now solve it. Attention will be paid to how fast you solve it."

Simple enough, I thought, looking at the pieces.

Then I noticed the instructor tugging out a fire hose from a box in the wall.

Wait a second. . . .

"Waterproof screens," Rakwon moaned.

I didn't even have time to swear. A powerful jet of frigid water knocked me back from my console. The carapoid instructor gleefully swept the stream of pounding water across the room. By the time I'd put the three-dimensional puzzle together, my fingers shook so hard I could barely manipulate the images.

To warm us all up, they ran us up and down the beach.

Last ones in didn't get dinner. So I went hungry again.

By lights-out I didn't have the energy to talk to Rakwon. But I did stop to drink enough water to get up early again.

Day three we built a tower out of large logs, and defended it against other teams on the beach. Ken led a team. He buried my face in the sand, choking me. "You're too slow to eat dinner. Chew on sand, coward," he hissed.

Maybe the girl with the purple hair had the right idea. I was going to have to kneecap Ken and get dragged away to a prison to get away from all this.

Rakwon and Cee Cee picked me up to brush the sand off.

I didn't want to meet Cee Cee's eyes. I felt half as tall as I was. But she joined Rakwon and me at breakfast again.

"It is what it is," Rakwon said philosophically, watching me glower. "Ken's officer bound. He's not worth the trouble."

"He's an asshole," I said. He was a collaborator.

But then, everyone here was a collaborator. Me too. I couldn't use that word out loud.

"He's excited to be here and he's well trained," Cee Cee said. "He's a good soldier. We're all ready to kick ass, right, recruit?"

I looked around. All of us in our grays. Training. Running. At Accordance's beck and call. I couldn't tell if Cee Cee was being sardonic or genuinely drinking it all in.

I kept my head down and mouth shut. I just needed to be adequate. So that my parents could live. So that I could survive this.

Just live through it, I told myself. Stay human.

On the fourth day, the mix of alien and human instructors started picking us off for interviews in small offices. I sat in front of a human instructor, a middle-aged man with graying hair and weary lines around his eyes. Behind him, a struthi-form instructor rustled feathers and glanced at a screen in his feathered, clawlike hands.

"We've been watching you," the human instructor said. "You're avoiding trouble. Following orders. Getting up early for breakfast: Nice trick with the water fountain. So, now it's time to think about how best you can be of use to the Colonial Protection Forces. How do you envision your future service?"

"I was thinking cook," I told them both. "Peeling potatoes.

Making stews. I could be a great sous-chef for the CPF, I think."

"Cook?" the alien asked.

"I've also heard some armies have bands, right? I used to play flute. . . ." I had the most earnest voice, and kept my face straight. But what else was I going to do? Ask them for the most dangerous position?

I just wanted to show up and do what I'd promised: no more, no less.

The human instructor cut me off. "You're not going to be in a band."

"There's a book in the indigenous literature section of the common library on this base," the struthiform said, craning its neck forward to regard me. "*Catch-22*. The concept behind the title is that you'd have to be crazy to ask for missions and sane if you didn't, but if you were sane you had to fight in the human war. But if you fought, that meant you were crazy, and shouldn't. And if you didn't want to fight, that meant you were sane and had to. See?"

I didn't. I hadn't read it, either. Most human classics had been not banned but "de-emphasized" in schools. There were older, superior Arvani sagas. And shows.

"You done having fun?" the human instructor asked. "Because here's the thing, recruit, it's all going to shit out there. And we're going to need all the bodies we can get."

He waved a hand. The desk between us filled with an orbital image of a world. Greenish clouds and unfamiliar, patchy continents.

"This is happening. Tens of light-years away. But as far as the Accordance is concerned, it's right next door and getting closer every day." The daylight faded; the planet spun into night.

Clusters of circular city lights in the planet's dark flickered. Then died. A cluster here, then another there. When the planet spun back into daylight, pillars of smoke streamed up to join the clouds.

The instructor swiped the image away. Flicked through videos of cities, unnaturally high Accordance spires and more black, treelike skyscrapers slumping over to the ground as their legs splintered and gave out. Bodies flicked by. Struthiforms, carapoids, a long-legged furry thing with surprisingly human-like eyes. The corpses lay still.

"We just lost an entire planet," the instructor said. Something large descended. Eldritch, asymmetrical, a city-sized jellyfish dropping out from the skies. Translucent, and yet it sucked all the light away as it moved.

"Conglomerate host-ship. Atmospheric entry class," the struthiform said coldly.

"Those black, flea-like things coating it, they're living ablative shields. They stick themselves onto the host-ship and use their backs to protect it as it enters the atmosphere. Once it's down, they detach and forage for food."

"Forage?" Millions of crispy shells fell clear of the shivering host-ship. Most broke as they struck the ground. The survivors, steaming hot, ripped into the corpses on the ground.

"The Accordance traced the home world of those creatures," the struthiform said. "They used to be a space-faring civilization. Intelligent. Now they're living heat shields. And that's it. Their monuments dust, their cities lost. Covered in a living shell of Conglomerate computational slurry that's slowly eating its way down into the core of their world. They reshape whole systems to their needs, and entire species to their whims. They love finding new biomes, like Earth's. They'll sample our DNA, investigate, catalog, and then reshape us into whatever they have a need for. They already tried this with the Pcholem once. That's why we need fighters, Devlin. Because we're losing worlds to them. We need more fighters."

The human instructor jumped back in. "Your test scores from the past few days are back. We think you're well suited for one particular arm of the Colonial Protection Forces."

I was still thinking about living ships discarding their heat shields to gobble alien corpses. "What do you think I'm so good at?"

"We're creating an all-human fighting force. Human officers. Human fighters. We need to build human expertise up, and stop depending on Accordance-led human squads so that we can grow the CPF's native strength. You're going to join the first all-human light enhanced infantry regiment."

Light enhanced infantry. Just enough powered armor that a human could keep up with enhanced infantry in the Accordance military. Just enough power that we would be put in the middle of alien-versus-alien action.

These two instructors sounded excited. As if I should be proud of the chance. I bet they sounded like this even when they were handing someone a toilet scrubber and explaining that the recruit's new mission would be to scrub toilets onboard an Accordance space station.

"There's a new training center on the dark side of the moon: Icarus. Named after the crater that surrounds the whole area it sits in," the human instructor said. "Congratulations, you ship out for Icarus tonight."

7

"Listen up!" drill instructors both alien and human shouted at us as we crowded together down on the cold morning beach. "You will bring nothing with you. You will leave all personal objects behind on this beach before getting inside transport craft."

Hoppers flew in over the Long Island Sound. They kicked up saltwater spray as they overflew the beach, and then dropped down to pick up recruits at the front of the line.

"Devlin!"

Rakwon and Cee Cee broke out of line, like many of us milling around the back, to say good-bye. It had been only a few days, and yet it felt like a graduation of some kind as we quickly hugged each other. "Where are you going?" I asked.

"Peacekeeper forces," Rakwon said. "Manhattan. If I keep in line, in a few years I could get a promotion."

"Peacekeeper? They gave me a whole big story about being desperate for soldiers in the CPF."

Rakwon shrugged. "They were talking about the 'repacification' process. We've been out of the news loop here all week. I think there are more riots or something. Well, at least I'll get to see my family on weekends. I can take a message to your family for you, if you want."

"No." They didn't want to hear from me. "What about you, Cee Cee?"

"Recruits: in line!" an instructor shouted.

"Orbital counterforces. Drones and links," Cee Cee shouted as she ran back to her place. "I might even get to fly a Stingray . . . if they pass the human pilots emergency authorization act."

"Good luck," Rakwon said as he ambled quickly away.

"No!" an all-too-familiar voice screamed from behind us all. We turned to see Ken dragged out through the doors and thrown into the sand. He staggered to his feet, lurching back toward the struthiform instructors that had thrown him out. His voice broke with emotion as he screamed, "You can't do this. This isn't how it's supposed to be! I'm from a Landed Family! I was born, and trained, to be an officer. Do you even know how much was invested in me?"

The nearest struthiform slapped him with the back of a feathery hand. Ken fell awkwardly into the sand. "Get in line," the alien snapped.

Ken crawled on his hands and knees, nose dripping blood down onto the sand. In just a single morning he'd fallen a long way from being the strutting leader of his instant crew. He crawled into line behind me, and someone helped him to his feet.

He looked at me with bruised eyes and a swelling lip. "You too?" he asked numbly.

"Light infantry," I confirmed, not quite sure whether I should enjoy his humiliation or hate the aliens that had back-handed him so casually. "I'm going to Icarus."

I wanted to ask if he was okay. But he very obviously wasn't. It was a stupid thing to want to ask. I didn't bother.

Ken swallowed. "You know what happens to human infantry."

"What?"

"We die."

The hoppers landed us at the flowerlike structures of the new Lakita Singh Air and Space Port. Instructors pushed and herded us into a launch terminal, then yelled at us some more.

"This is your buddy," a human instructor said. He shoved a nervous recruit at me. "Put your hand on your buddy's shoulder. Hold tight. Now, you are responsible for your buddy. Anything happens to your buddy, it'll happen to you. When I ask you where your buddy is, you won't tell me, because you'll be holding your buddy's shoulder and it'll be so obvious where he is, you won't have to say anything. Got it?"

I nodded.

The instructor shook his head, like my father when trying to teach me some complex piece of math that I just couldn't quite get the first time around. "You don't nod. You answer with a 'yes' and an 'instructor' in there, son. The Hamptons may be run by aliens that don't allow us to use 'sir,' but we can work around that. You're still CPF. And it'll be all-human CPF for you lot. So my rules apply. Let's try that again: got it?"

"Yes . . . instructor!" I fumbled. His eyes narrowed, then he nodded and moved on to the next recruit.

"What's your name?" my shoulder buddy asked. We were standing awkwardly facing each other, an arm each on a shoulder, like at a dance.

"Devlin. You?"

"Keiko."

We'd been lined up against the walls of the terminal. This was a wing for launches headed for orbit, not flights around the world. Since the occupation, the Accordance had dismantled most of the smaller airline hubs in favor of incredibly high-speed rail. But international flights and flights to space were still served.

LSP had once been something else, before the aliens had deemed it unusable and demolished it. Another set of letters. "At least," my father had told me, "they kept a human name on the port."

Most of the humans in the port flaunted expensive suits and waited in glassed-off areas with subdued lighting. They sat on lounge chairs where attendants came by to take their orders. We watched them eat, laugh, and sashay around.

Someone pushed a pink dog in a stroller back and forth across the waiting area, cooing at it, feeding it tiny snacks.

The hushed, quiet space behind that glass could have been mine. I could have been mixing with those upper-class civilians, enjoying finger food and traveling the world. If I hadn't thrown away my usefulness as a propaganda tool.

Now . . . I rubbed my short hair.

What was taking so long? We'd been just sitting here for twenty minutes, hands on shoulders, bored.

"Look at that," Keiko said with wonder in his voice. "I saw her get hauled off for beating a kid up. You saw that, right?"

I leaned far forward. At the very end of the line the girl with silver eyes and still-purple hair sat on the ground as two human instructors conferred over her.

"*Smell* that," I said, my attention drifting across the hall as my stomach growled.

For those in a hurry, a Brooklyn brownstone had been pulled apart, brick by brick, and painstakingly reassembled in the terminal. And on the steps, in front of it, an "authentic" food cart sold hot dogs and cheeseburgers.

"Did you get a chance to eat before getting shoved out to the beach?" Keiko asked.

"No," I said. "Look, we're about to be shot off to who the hell knows where. We've been drinking balls of juice in round slime containers. Because it's optimal and easy to feed us that way. This might be our last chance to eat something real for a long, long time."

"We have to stay put," Keiko said. "They'll kill us. . . ."

I looked down the line. The instructors were still focused on paperwork and the purple-haired girl. "Last chance," I hissed. "Even if I get in trouble: It'll be all on me. I promise, it'll be worth it."

Recruits on either side had been listening in. "Just grab my shoulder when he goes," someone suggested.

"How you gonna pay?" someone else asked.

I glanced back down the line. The instructors had their backs to me. I let go of Keiko.

"Shit, man, don't do this," he whined.

I lit out away from the group, quickly, just to get distance. Then I walked casually over. "Hey," I called out.

The older lady at the cart looked startled. Her blue eyes darted back and forth. "I can't help you run, son," she hissed. "It's humans-only in this terminal anyway, you can't go any-where without passing a checkpoint."

"No," I spread my hands. "This is our last chance to get any real food. Before . . ."

She let out a deep breath.

"Look, my father's name is Thomas Hart. I don't have any

way to pay on me, they took everything away, but if you contact him, he'll . . ."

"What do you want?" she asked quickly. She just wanted to get rid of me, I realized.

"Anything I can carry," I said quickly. She slid me a box of doughnuts and five hot dogs on a cardboard tray. I eased back across into the line.

"Holy shit, holy shit," Keiko hissed as I slid back into line. "Holy shit."

"Come on. Pass these along. Hurry up! Drop the box on the floor when we're done, put a doughnut in your pocket, a hot dog in the other." I stuffed my hot dog into my mouth.

Oh man. Never had street food tasted . . . So. Fucking. Good.

"Move on up!" the instructors shouted, turning around, their paperwork done. Actually, no, I realized: A struthiform instructor had arrived. The human instructors had been waiting for the real leadership to show up.

The doughnut scraped sugar on the outside of my pocket, but I wiped it off best I could.

"Let's go! Keep it moving! Get aboard the jumpship." I chewed my hot dog surreptitiously as I passed the instructors waving us through down to our new transport.

The wedge-shaped jumpship's blistered and pockmarked skin, which I'd glimpsed near the docking tube, meant it had seen quite a few reentries. There were no portholes, no screens. Just ribbed metal hull and foam seats for us. Two carapoid pilots sat behind a bulkhead and door, however. They shut it as we entered.

"Buckle in. You should know how to use a buckle. So get it done already! You, sit. Sit there. With your buddy."

Minutes later the ship rose through the air. I could feel engine pods under our feet, and then even heavier Accordance engines kicking on behind us. This was no hopper. The engines behind us growled with energy and shoved us back into our seats. Manhattan's Accordance-spired skyline fell away as we tilted toward the clouds and flew up.

With alacrity. The pressure of acceleration continued to press on my chest. Whenever I thought the squeezing had to stop, it continued to press harder.

Until, with a gasp, it went away.

Weightlessness. A big smile grew on my face, despite myself. There were no portholes, but I knew we were in orbit. I knew that from here, if I could see anything, I'd be looking down at the continents and the curve of the Earth.

"What *the fuck* is this?" an instructor asked, unbuckling herself to rise up into the air to grab at something.

It was a doughnut, trailing sugar glaze in the air.

"What is unauthorized food doing on *my* transport?" the instructor shouted. Her ponytailed hair bobbed behind her as she looked around. "Who did this?"

She only got a series of blank looks from my row.

Another instructor bounced up into the air. "Don't anyone unbuckle. We're going to search you. . . ."

Ken raised a hand. "Instructor: I know!"

"Rat motherfucker," I hissed. I barely had time to say even that. One very angry instructor's face was right up in mine as she positioned herself in the air next to me.

Then the other.

The yelling began, and behind them, Ken held up a doughnut of his own and took a bite with a big smile.

It looked like his natural state of asshole had come back online.

Everyone poured excitedly out of the docking tube into Tranquility City. "Hey. Gravity," someone said.

"I can't bounce around like those old astronaut videos. What gives?"

"Antigravity in the floors," Ken announced. "When my family visited Tranquility, they told us humans aren't allowed dense attractor technology."

"Antigravity," someone chimed in.

"Dense. Attractor. Technology," Ken repeated.

That was why the one human space station struggling in orbit still had people floating around in it. And our transport, a cheap craft used to move recruits around, had none either.

But somewhere underfoot, Accordance engineers had laid down a grid of material that pulled us all down toward it. Immensely expensive, and done just so that they could be comfortable here on the moon.

The cargo bay's vaulted ceilings stretched far overhead, like a giant's ribcage. Robotic forklifts with long, articulated, spiderlike arms scurried around the football-sized open floor,

pulling square containers off five-story racks that they sometimes had to climb up to reach.

"I saw a whole program about the people they flew to the
moon to do the construction," Keiko said. This part of the city
had been dug out by humans helping run alien-built mining
machines. The end of the cargo bay was a massive airlock
designed for giants, with train tracks running through it into
the bay.

"Okay recruits, keep walking!"

We trooped out of the busy cargo bay in obedient lines
and snaked our way into Tranquility City's subways and
tunnels. Then up a series of escalators, everyone still making
sure to keep a hand on the shoulder of the recruit in front of
them.

The familiar architecture of Accordance spires appeared
when we broke street level.

"Fuck me," Keiko said. "We're on the surface of the moon."

"Keep moving!" the instructors shouted as we stumbled,
looking around.

"Nothing like on a screen," I said, awed and also stumbling
after the recruit in front of me.

Translucent material capped the streets between buildings,
letting us look up into the black sky. Bright light dripped from
luminescent globes and strips, filling shadows and crevices
with a soft green light to augment the natural sunlight. Gray
hills circled around the city where the streets ended, plunging
back underground.

"I thought I'd see stars," someone said.

"Too much light. Washes it out. Just like at a stadium."

"It's Earth," Keiko whispered as we turned the gentle curve
of an Accordance skyscraper's base.

It hung in the sky, blue and small. Everyone stopped as

they looked up. The entire line bunched into a crowd. I craned my neck, ignoring the busy street.

"What's that?" someone else asked. A comet-like silver shape high overhead occluded the Earth briefly, casting us in a flitting shadow before moving on.

"A Pcholem ship," someone said. "They came in those ships."

"That *is* a Pcholem. Not a ship. Pcholem."

"What?"

"Move!" a struthiform instructor hissed, coming up along-side us. "Move now."

Carapoids moved around us on the street, and more struthi-forms bobbed past to avoid us. The streets ran thick with aliens going about their business. Several water-filled glass bubbles with Arvani inside trundled past.

"It's just us," Keiko said. "We're the only humans out here."

Most humans on the moon worked for the Helium-3 mines, or on Accordance construction.

We kept moving, still looking up for a last glimpse of home, until we passed under another large airlock at the city's edges. Humans glanced at us from several small eateries that lined the edge of the oval common area.

No shiny, green-tinged metal cleaning robots in here. Trash and dirt littered the crosswalks and graffiti filled the walls.

Welcome to the human section.

"I gotta go," Keiko whispered.

"What?"

"Bathroom. We're in a human zone, right? I gotta go."

"The instructors are out for my blood already, now we're going to get noticed again?"

"That's not fair," Keiko said. "As your buddy, I'm going to catch all that shit too. So the least you can do is help me take a dump."

I groaned as Keiko raised a hand and waved.

"What is it?" the nearest instructor asked, her ponytail whipping around.

"I need to use a bathroom, instructor."

"Buddy up. The nearest one is right across the museum. You have ten minutes. If you're not aboard . . ." She let the missing words hang in the air.

I wondered what they did to recruits absent without leave here on the moon. The Accordance owned it outright, now. It didn't belong to humans anymore, even though they could see Tranquility City's lights from Earth.

Humans hadn't been using the planets and their moons, the Accordance had noted. It was better they be developed by a civilization actually able to do so. It would happen anyway. That was the stick. The carrot was the offer to keep autonomy by signing off.

On Earth, humans still demanded the right to run themselves directly despite occupation, and would cause trouble to keep that. Here? The Accordance could do anything they wanted.

Be careful up here, I thought. Make it out the other side.

"Where's the museum, instructor?" Keiko asked.

She pointed between the restaurants across from us. Hand on shoulder, Keiko and I crossed the hundred yards of common area.

The Apollo Cultural Heritage Preservation Site. The pictures I'd seen had never shown it surrounded by a pair of restaurants filled with tired-looking lunar miners in overalls.

On the other side of the translucent doors I saw a familiar boxy shape.

Keiko made a strangled sound. "Bathrooms, here we go." Right outside the museum, between the nearest restaurant and the museum.

"I'm going to let go of your shoulder now," I said.

"Yeah, whatever." He scurried inside, and I heard a stall bang shut.

And just on the other side of the wall from where he squatted, something that took humanity decades to create gathered dust in an exhibit. The pinnacle of achievement in outer space. The farthest a human had ever gone from our world. The Apollo Lunar Module descent stage.

The Accordance had crossed stars. We had made it to the moon.

Keiko clamped his hand on my shoulder and I yelped. "You look deep in thought," he said.

"Yeah, well."

We crossed back. "What were you thinking so hard on? How much we're going to kick ass at training camp?"

I opened my mouth to answer, but the response never came. A wave of hot energy smacked into the back of my head with a roar. The explosion came a split second later. Or, at least, my awareness of it did.

Things spun around me until my head smacked into the steel-and-concrete ground.

Everything faded. I lay still, blinking and looking at the world askew.

The roar hadn't stopped. It kept thundering on. A wind rushed past me up toward the ceiling. I wiped blood on my sleeves and twisted around. "Keiko?" I croaked.

People ran past us, trying to get through the ten-foot-thick doors that trundled toward each other to seal off the human section. They dodged chunks of metal and dirty moon concrete and just barely slid through.

A flurry of sharp dust whipped around, stinging my throat as I tried to pull in a deep breath.

"Recruits: on board, now!" an instructor shouted. "In, in, in!"

"Keiko!" I staggered back in the direction I'd been tossed from and away from the airlock where the instructor stood. "Keiko."

"Recruit!"

I glanced back. No gray shapes stood in line anymore. They'd all boarded. Gotten safely inside the craft that would take us to our training camp. If I ran there, I might make it in. They would have to shut the door soon, to stop losing air.

Because that was what the wind was: air getting sucked out of the cracked top of the human section. It had been half-buried under one of the hills surrounding Tranquility City, where all the rock and dirt came from.

Keiko lay next to a chunk of roof, a pool of blood slowly spreading around him. I scrabbled over. A supporting beam the size of a car had pinned his leg, bent it, and trapped him in place.

I saw white bone when I looked underneath. And more blood. It kept pulsing out the ruined mangle of flesh.

He stirred slightly, a moan of pain, but his glassy eyes looked through me as I grabbed his bloody hand and squeezed it. "Hold on!" I shouted. "Just hold on."

I panted and blinked, dizzy and coughing in the dust still whipping around me. How could I stop the bleeding? We didn't have belts, and there was so much damn blood.

And I could barely focus. Or breathe.

Hands behind me pushed a mask against my face. "Take a deep breath."

"Okay. . . ." I turned. Silvered eyes, purple hair. Behind a similar emergency rebreathing mask.

"What's your name?" she asked.

"Devlin," I murmured. Then stronger as oxygen cleared my head. "Devlin!"

"I'm Amira." She kicked off one of her boots and unlaced

it. "Give him air too. You take a couple of pulls, give it to him for a couple."

"Right." My senses rushed back as my brain got moving again. Three deep breaths, then I got the mask on Keiko. "Do you know what to do?"

"I'm reading instructions right now," she said, voice muffled behind the rebreather.

The eyes. The nano-ink tattoos. Like Cee Cee, she could ride invisible bandwidth. A hacker. Full of bioware and other computing and neural hardware. She'd be pulling up entries on how to stop bleeding and following the instructions. I took two pulls on the rebreather, then set it back on Keiko's face. I couldn't tell if he was breathing; there was no fog on the glass visor.

"Hands up!" came an order shouted so loud my ears buzzed. Struthiforms in thick, full-black armor and helmets ran at us. "Hands up, don't move."

Amira was trying to get the shoelace around Keiko's thigh and cinch it. Blood soaked the lace, and her fingers dripped red. I moved in front of her and Keiko, my bloody hands in the air. "We're CPF recruits!" I shouted into the thin air. "We need medical attention for—"

The head struthiform in the wedge formation struck me with a wing hand. I crumpled to the ground, dizzied by the hit. It held my face down in Keiko's muddied blood as another Accordance soldier zip-tied my hands.

"If you continue to struggle, you will be shot."

"I don't understand," I gasped, the dizziness creeping back over me. "We're CPF. Why are you doing this?"

Amira looked over, her face also shoved into the ground. "It was a bomb. A human bomb. All humans in Tranquility are getting arrested."

9

Amira wriggled her shoulders, stretched, and then pulled free of the zip tie. She rubbed her wrists and put the tie on the table between us.

"How did you do that?" I asked.

"Isn't your dad Thomas Hart?"

"Yeah."

"And he didn't teach you to cross your wrists and flex before getting zip-tied? Or how to break them off?"

"We never fought the arrests," I told her. The struthiforms that interrogated me in a separate room had retied my hands in front of me. I held them toward her now. "Can you help?"

"I will. But when they are about to come back, you need to put them back on, got it?"

"Definitely. I'll keep them loose around my wrists."

She pushed a fingernail in and somehow released the catch. The tie opened up, and I massaged my hands. "Thank you. Thank you for coming over."

"You looked ready to pass out," she said. "The rebreather

masks were in a locker near the transport's airlock. Didn't feel right watching you die."

I looked down at the brown flakes on my fingers, and on hers. "Did you get the shoelace tied before they pulled us away?"

Amira waited a beat. "No."

"He wasn't breathing." I refused to look up at her. I kept my head down.

"I know."

I took a deep breath. "I didn't go to any regular schools much, we moved too often. I've been in the middle of protests, riots, arrests. I've seen people shot, but carried away by ambulances quickly. I've never seen that much blood before. It's like something from San Francisco."

"Or earlier," Amira said, somewhat nonchalantly. "Before your dad. When the fighting was violent. The paramedics couldn't get in during Pacification."

"You're not *that* much older than me," I said. "You were, what, eight or nine years old then?"

"Yes," she said.

I imagined a young Amira watching a running gun battle in the middle of a burned-out New Jersey. "And now you're fighting for the Accordance?"

Amira's jaw clenched. "Your parents are still alive and resisting. Lucky you. Mine were executed on a street corner. I survived because if you needed a pass, a way into limited movement areas, then you had to talk to little Amira Singh. For a payment I'd help hack and forge anything. My parents had wanted me to help the cause. The whole family invested in the cost of me taking online classes and apprenticing to older hackers, but all those investors had hungry children who needed me as a meal ticket after their parents were shot. Lucky for them I learn fast. Lucky for them I had the education. Unlucky for them, now, that I've been dragged off and they have no one."

She waved her fingers over her eyes and at the silvered swirls on her arms and neck. "Accordance isn't supposed to sell this on Earth, but there are always black markets where less-than-scrupulous aliens can make money selling us what we can't make ourselves. I can tap into Accordance virtual networks and augmented reality feeds. We'll never be full citizens, but I can at least taste a little of their world. When they caught up to me they gave me a choice: a lifetime sentence, or the CPF. *That's* why I'm here."

"I'm sorry."

"Fuck 'sorry.' Everyone's sorry the Accordance invaded our world. I'm sorry half my neighborhood fought back. Sorry I detected enforcers coming and hid myself, but couldn't warn the rest of my family. We're sorry that kid died in front of us. I'll bet you're sorry you betrayed your parents to serve in the CPF."

She leaned forward and pulled her zip tie closed with her teeth as I stared at her.

"Someone's coming?" I asked, doing the same.

"Under emergency session, acting president Barnett just forced microchip legislation through," Amira said, letting go of the tie. "Everyone is now going to be sorry that Tranquility was bombed by radicals, because if they want to travel, they'll now need to be tagged like the little pets we are. Everyone's fucking sorry, Devlin. It's the state of the universe these days. But at least you tried to help someone next to you, and that's more than we often get."

The door slid open. An Arvani commander in full matte-black battle gear scuttled through the door. Its eight mecha-nized tentacles tapped the ground as it approached us.

No water in a tank, like civilian Arvani. This armor form-fitted the alien. Pistons and plates hugged the octopus-like form, sliding and shifting with it as it walked toward us.

Shimmering glass covered the large, unblinking eyes. "Call me Commander Zeus. The sound is close to what I like to think my name begins with, and I hear the name holds import, so I will have it. I'm your new instructor. Of all the indignities piled on me of late, my latest is that all the human instructors at the Icarus camp have been dismissed and your training turned over to me. I had to come pick you apes up myself.

"If I could, I'd leave you here to rot. But that would be more paperwork than just hauling myself down here to drag you out of this room. Let's move."

Commander Zeus turned around.

"No," I said, refusing to get up.

The commander pivoted back, a scary rapid uncoiling movement that happened in the blink of an eye, and regarded me. "No?"

"Tell me what happened to Keiko."

The Arvani didn't move for a second. "Dead."

I'd expected that. I didn't expect it to suck the air out of me even though I'd prepared for it.

"We need to do something," I said. I wasn't sure what. Some kind of ceremony. Something.

Zeus knocked the chair out from under me. I hit the ground with a groan, and the commander squatted over me. "One dead recruit is a tiny speck of shit in a whirlpool," the alien said. "There will be more before your time is over. This is the perspective you should curl your limbs around."

"We still have to respect our fallen," I said. "It's what we do."

"The fallen do not care," Commander Zeus said. "And I do not care 'what you do.' But I will tell you what *I* will do. If you do not follow me out of this room, there will be consequences for your dereliction. I'm sure you can imagine them. I do not care what you choose. My duty to protocol here has been made."

Zeus turned around.

Amira grabbed my arm and helped me up.

"Remember Keiko in your own way," she said. "Let it go for now. Don't put you or your family on the list."

"I had to—"

"I know. But you just pissed off Captain Calamari there. The creature that'll be running our whole world for the next few weeks."

"Commander Calamari," I corrected her.

"No." Amira squinted. "I think it's Captain Calamari for me."

10

The commander's tentacles filled most of the free space in the tiny craft that dropped out of the lunar night, leaving Amira and me to push ourselves as far up against the back bench as we could.

Through the large porthole on my side I watched as we arced high over the cratered mountains in the dark, whipping a mile overhead a desolate landscape punctuated by the occasional grid and piping of lunar mining facilities.

There were so many craters. The Earth-facing side of the moon had been smoother with its seas and plains. The dark side looked as if it had been in a long, losing war: billions of years of constant artillery bombardment, ravaged by the vengeance of outer space's constant barrage of rocks from beyond Earth's orbit.

All around me, as far as I could see right now, was the Icarus crater. It was almost sixty miles wide, and we'd been flying over it for the last couple minutes.

"Big railgun," Amira said. I looked out her porthole. A mile-long bridge-like structure ran along the surface. It held a long pipe in its struts rather than a road, though. "A mining facility. They're taking the processed ore chunks and just shooting them in capsules to wherever in orbit they need to go for Accordance projects."

As we watched, lights danced up and down the trusses and a capsule slightly bigger than the craft we sat in hurtled toward the horizon and rose up into orbit.

A minute or two later, another one followed it.

"Your new home." Commander Zeus tapped an armored tip against the curved screen in front of him.

The lights of the Icarus training facility lit up the horizon, then almost blinded me as we crested a hill. The craft shuddered as the commander fired engines to slow our forward motion to a near stop, leaving us hanging just over the complex.

Below us an entire crater had been capped with a clear dome, then filled with ponds, brush, bridges, obstacle courses, and other objects I couldn't identify.

Four petal-shaped complexes spread out around the capped dome, making it look like a giant clover from above. More half-buried cylinders popped up inside nearby craters.

"The dome allows for a variety of conditions," Commander Zeus explained. "We can heat it, chill it, raise the pressure, lower it. Blow wind. Flood it. Put in any number of atmospheres from a variety of planets. We can create storms, hail, winter, summer. We can change the gravity itself via dense attractor base plates buried under the ground. Your living quarters are off to the sides, your commanders live in the quarters one crater over. Be proud: We invested a lot in this for just humans."

We gently struck a landing pad on top of one of the petals. It pulled us inside, the roof closing overhead after it.

The pad came to a shuddering halt near a row of rovers, their massive balloon-like wheels almost touching each other.

"You're just in time," the commander said. "While you've spent a day sitting around doing nothing, your teammates have had a meal, learned where their rooms are, and are getting ready for their first round of Escape the School."

"Escape the School?" Amira asked.

"I'm told it's a rough translation of a concept we Arvani use in our training. I want to see you all in action."

Recruits strung out in a circle in the natural amphitheater to the back of the capped lunar dome.

We slipped in at the back of the line, taking our place. Most of the recruits were in their late teens, like me. Quite a few in their twenties, though. "War's a young man's game," my father had often said. "One where older statesmen send the patriotic young to settle their elders' disagreements with their blood."

I looked around. Lots of thickly muscled arms and strong backs. I felt like the runt in the back. Whatever came next, I guessed I'd have to depend on quick feet and quick thinking.

Commander Zeus descended on a cabled platform from the top of the dome.

He threw a black ball out with one of his tentacles into the muddy grass in front of the recruits. "The moment your fingerprints touch the ball," he shouted, "it registers that you have possession. It also lights up so you can't hide with it."

We all regarded the ball.

"The aim of this test is to show me who can hold on to the ball the longest."

Someone raised a hand. "What happens to those who hold it the shortest? Or who don't get it at all?"

"Your orders," Zeus said, "are to hold on to it the longest."

Amira stood behind me, her arms folded. "You remember the beach on the Hamptons?" I asked her. "We need to get our hands on that thing. Together."

"One against everyone is going to be hell," she agreed. "A bunch of us against everyone else is going to be more survivable."

"Right. Let's find anyone we know."

We started walking around, looking for recruits we recognized from the trip to Tranquility City.

The platform began to rise back up into the air on its cables, lifting Zeus into a catwalk gallery under the dome.

"One last change in the current," the alien commander shouted. "I will be venting the dome's atmosphere until you pass out to see how you function."

I thought about the choking moon dust lacerating my throat as I struggled to breathe back in Tranquility City.

"Hey, it's Doughnuts," a voice called out. Amira pulled a familiar-looking dark-haired recruit along.

"Nico's in," she said.

"What are the rules?" a recruit down the line shouted up at the retreating platform. It was Ken, I realized. "What are we allowed to do?"

There was no reply.

Amira yanked more people over to me. Our hasty team grabbed shoulders in a huddle. I counted ten of us, mostly all recognizable from the ride to the moon. "Here's the idea," I said. "If any of us can grab it, the rest of us huddle around and protect them. We rotate in, get some holding time, until we've all got hands on it. Then we let it go. Yell 'ball' and we'll surround you. Each of us gets five seconds."

"You sure this will work?" the recruit who'd nicknamed me Doughnuts asked.

"No," I said. "We'll get the shit kicked out of us trying to do it. But you think it'll go any better with us trying it alone?"

A horn blared, an unmistakable start signal.

A scrum instantly developed over the ball. Individuals scrapping around the mud to try to hold on. Legs churned, bodies writhed.

One of the recruits staggered out of the mass of bodies, swore, then threw herself back in with a vicious elbow to someone's neck.

"My finger's broken! Help!" A scraggly boy crawled out and held up a hand. Bone stuck out of the side of his finger and blood ran down his wrist.

But no help came down from the gantry. Or from anywhere else.

Ken approached us, a surprisingly humble nervousness obvious in his body language. "Create a wedge," he said. "I think that'll get us in there."

"There is no '*us,*'" I snarled at him, remembering his elbow digging into the back of my neck as he shaved my head, embarrassing me in front of Cee Cee.

He raised his hands, conciliatory. "Look, I'm sorry about the doughnuts."

"Fuck off," I said, and turned my back. I took several deep breaths, watching the dozens of recruits in front of us fighting like a cluster of weasels over the ball. I glanced back and saw Ken walking away, looking for someone else to join forces with.

"We need all the help we can get," Amira muttered to me.

"Fuck him. We don't need *his* help."

"He was right about wedging in," Amira said.

I grunted. "I guess."

"When do we try for it?" the guy who'd called me Dough-nuts asked.

I looked over at Amira's silver eyes. "Our instructors are venting air. When do we start getting dizzy?"

The right corner of her mouth pulled back, a half smile as she figured out what I was thinking. The first time I'd seen that. "Five minutes. More or less."

"I want to eat dinner first tonight, if they're pulling that stunt from the Hamptons again," I said. "So we're just going to stand here and take long, deep breaths. Keep yourself oxygenated. We're going to form up in a triangle, and keep our arms locked together. Biggest up at the spear tip, right? If that scrum moves at all, we slowly track it. Amira, can you keep time for us?"

"Nice thinking, Doughnuts."

"It's Devlin," I said. "You are?"

"Grayson."

We linked arms and formed up, like protestors facing an advancing line of enforcers. The hard part would be waiting and holding as Amira ticked off a minute, and then another. I kept up a running patter of positive support, keeping the small squad upbeat about our plan.

"Three minutes," she reported. The scrum broke apart. A recruit with a ripped uniform punched someone in the face and tore free. Blood streamed down his face as he held the ball to his barrel-like chest, cradled in thick, muscular arms. The ball lit up like a small sun as he placed his fingers against it. We all blinked and shielded our eyes.

"Let's get him," Grayson said. We all surged forward a bit.

"Walk!" I shouted. "Walk. Stay together."

A cloud of recruits surged after the recruit with the ball. They ran across the mud toward an obstacle course away from the open clearing we'd assembled in.

Some of the runners looked woozy, but determined.

"Two minutes," Amira called out.

"Breathe deep, walk easy," I said as we shuffled after the prize.

The recruit finally succumbed to the crowds chasing him and went down. The scrum reassembled, occasional figures wrapping themselves around the ball in a fetal position as they got the shit kicked out of them and the ball pried out of their hands.

"One minute."

Screams of injured recruits echoed off the dome and bounced back down at us. I glanced up at the catwalk. Zeus stood on his platform, surveying the chaos but not putting a stop to it.

"It's sleepy time," Amira said.

"Go!" I shouted.

Our wedge struck the scrum hard, scattering bodies and trampling people caught by surprise. We were fresh, not dizzy, and organized.

"Get the ball but don't unlink your arms!" Amira shouted.

"Count to five, then pass it along." I hoped that whoever had snagged it wouldn't hog it, or I'd be screwed.

The center of our huddle lit up, dazzling my eyes as one of the recruits managed to get on his knees to retrieve the ball. Behind me, a knee struck my kidney hard enough that I sagged in place as I gasped.

I hung limp, tears running down my cheeks. Amira yanked me back onto my feet.

"Pass."

The ball was passed to the right as we huddled and weathered a storm of scratches, punches, and attempts to pierce our human wall.

But the air loss was having an affect. The punches were weaker. The roars of rage choked. We were on our knees, arms still linked, heads together, struggling to keep strong.

When Amira awkwardly passed me the ball I hugged it to

my stomach. At the count of four, the Klaxon sounded. We all flopped onto our backs and gasped fresh air as it streamed back into the dome in a rush of wind.

Commander Zeus descended from the sky on the platform, picked around the passed-out humans—sidestepping moaning recruits being tended to by struthiform medics—and ignored the still-standing survivors who eyed him warily.

"I seem to have been stuck with a mass of miserably performing apes!" the Arvani commander shouted. "And while I find you all about as appealing as barnacle growth, I have my duty. So we have a lot of work to do."

I didn't like the sound of that.

Zeus paused in front of me. "You: You performed tolerably. You will pick seven to create your arm."

"My what?"

"Your arm," Zeus repeated. "A collection of fighters. Eight fighters to an arm. You will be their octave."

"Sounds like we're going to be a group of fighting flutists," Amira muttered behind me.

Zeus raised the voice coming from the armor. "Eventually there will be twenty-five arms here on the base. You will learn to lead your arm, and the arms will also learn to fight together and against each other. It is a privilege to be an octave. Grasp it tightly. Hurry to pick your team, or the other octaves will have their choices."

"Amira," I called out.

Zeus moved across the mud. "You: You are an octave."

I didn't pay attention to who the other octaves were. "Grayson." He could keep calling me Doughnuts if he wanted, but he'd held the line.

"Worst game of playground dodgeball ever," he muttered, but came to stand next to me.

I started grabbing recruits, some from our group, others that I'd noticed who'd somehow grabbed time on the ball during the exercise.

Amira tapped me on the shoulder as our team formed. "You have a fan," she said.

Ken stood near a climbing wall, his arm in an inflatable cast and a purple welt over his right eye. He glowered at us, then pointed a finger at a tall recruit. She jogged over to join his team.

Ken pointed at me and flipped me off.

"Family privilege," I grunted. "Welcome to Earth under the occupation. Apparently he gets to be an octave whether he's skilled or not."

Amira raised an eyebrow. "You sure about that?" she asked.

I was.

"Hurry up and pick your team, know-it-all," she murmured. "Pay attention, there are some people you don't want Ken to snag from under you."

11

I had yet to see my bunk, but I guess it didn't matter. I didn't come to Icarus with any belongings. I didn't have anything to put down anywhere.

Zeus clanked his way around the warehouse we'd been ushered to in one of the living quarters off the crater dome, deep in one of the cloverleaf-like areas, eyeing the various arms assembled before him.

"Now that the arms are picked and the octaves are in command, you will suit up in armor," Zeus announced.

My arm shifted, its members slightly excited by the announcement.

I had picked Grayson Stockton, from Leeds, who played rugby before getting recruited out of a tenement in occupied London. He'd literally held me up while we fought for the ball. Another member of the first team, Casimir Sharpe, I'd spotted moving quickly through the mess before he joined us. I wanted that speed on my side.

Amira had pointed out a Viking shield-maiden of a figure towering over half the group near the back. "You'll want

Amabel there for muscle," she said. "The other octaves aren't taking her seriously."

"Yeah." If Amira wanted her, she was with us.

Roger Li, another member of our initial huddle, agreed to come with us. Haselda Madsen was another Amira suggestion. "I sat next to her on the way to Tranquility. She's smart."

"Smart is good," I said.

"She's also spent time in Brazil and Chile. With Roger's Mandarin, you have two of the most common CPF first languages outside of English. The Accordance is pulling a lot of different people together, and that means we have a variety of languages being used. A lot of them know English as a second language, but we can't count on it. There'll be a lot of Chinese-, Indian-, and Spanish-speaking recruits."

Zeus raised an armor-plated tentacle. "Your armor," he announced.

Struthiform officers pushed racks of black armor into the room, the suits swaying on their hooks. Each suit split open, looking like mandibles of black, chitinous insects ready to swallow us.

We stared. The sleek plating and mechanized joints meant this was Accordance military-grade issue. Designed for humans, but illegal on Earth. Even human enforcers didn't get to step into this stuff.

"Check out the patches on the shoulder," Amira said. "At least that's human designed."

A stylized Earthrise had been etched into each shoulder patch. The pockmarked moon in the foreground, Earth rising behind it.

"What are you gawping at?" Zeus shouted. "Get suited up!"

"How?" I asked, tentatively approaching the cracked-open suits.

"Some on-our-feet learning," Amira said.

"Oh, come on." Amabel laughed. "I've seen struthiforms do this on-base outside Charleston when I was four. We'd sneak up to the edge of the base and watch them train." She strode over, spun around, and put out her arms. Then backed into a hanging suit.

The cuffs snapped to her wrists, legs snapped forward, and the chest closed in. The whole suit gripped her and sealed shut with a hiss, seams disappearing. It readjusted, shaping itself with minor tweaks until it conformed to her size and shape.

She winced. "Okay, that hurts a little."

"What hurts?" Casimir asked, a little nervously.

Amabel raised her legs, rocking back and forth on the hook. "Come find out," she challenged.

I walked forward. The suit was alien. Inside I could see the lay of the cut-open human shape it manifested, but that was the only recognizable human element of the suit. The interior of the suit glowed with spiky filaments of some kind of bio-luminescent mold.

I turned around and backed in.

When my arms touched the gauntlets, they startled me by grabbing my wrists. The rest of the suit snapped shut around me, just like Amabel's had.

Sections readjusted shape, memory metal shifting and pulling in tight to become a heavy second skin. Something pricked my skin, then shoved its way into my lower back. The burning sensation spread up my spine.

I gasped. "That's invasive."

Around me the rest of the arm backed into their suits until we all dangled from hooks.

Zeus moved to the front of the mess. "This is a fusion of inferior human technology and the superior workmanship of the Cal Riata."

"The what?" someone closer to the front asked.

"Arvani that left the depths for the shallows," Zeus told us. "We colonized the lakes and tidal pools of the Arv. We did that by building machines to let us explore land. We are still the leaders of Arvani invention and study. You should consider yourselves honored that I'm stuck here in your backwater."

"He sound a little bitter about being here to you?" Amira asked.

"Hard to tell, the voice is synthesized; but I think you're right," Amabel said.

"This armor," Zeus shouted, drowning out the snapping sound of the suits closing up, "is powered by the same engines as a hopper, just smaller. It can do more than just increase your strength five times over: It features adaptive real-time camouflage, and it can recycle the internal air for a few days as well as liquids for up to a week."

"Ewww." Grayson made a face.

"Your communications have quantum entanglement for security on each arm's own channel, entangled again for a connection back to Command. There are also public radio frequencies for inter-arm—"

A loud crash interrupted Zeus. Someone had leapt off his hook and buried himself in the ceiling. The soft material rained to the floor, and the recruit had obviously not died as he kicked and wiggled around, stuck in the gooey ceiling. Obviously the room was designed with a safety feature.

Zeus didn't look up, just waited a second and then continued. "First, you need to visualize your helmet. This finishes the suit-up process now that there is a neural link with your spinal cord."

I closed my eyes and thought about a helmet. The rim snicked and then something thunked into place. The air around my head filled with the sound of my breathing. I opened my eyes to see the helmet had shot out of the collar and surrounded my head.

"And now I'll release the suits from their racks," Zeus said, his voice filling my helmet. "Move slowly, and cautiously. Do not damage my ceiling any further."

The hook yanked free, and I stumbled forward. Each step jerked oddly, but as I took each one, something about the suit seemed to stop resisting and then overreacting to me. It began to move with me. Anticipate my movements.

By my tenth step, I felt one with the suit and no longer like an awkward toddler staggering forward.

"Hey, this is Amira." Amira's voice startled me by filling the helmet as well. "I know you're all new to this, but just think about where you want to talk to. Think 'Command' and you'll be sending to Zeus. Probably not a good idea unless you have to. Think of your team, or arm I mean, and you'll be on the channel."

Then right over, Zeus came in. "Now it's time to get used to your suits."

A few groans popped out on the public channel from other arms.

Zeus scuttled out of the room and we followed. Down halls, and then out into the domed crater we'd struggled through earlier.

There were no days on the moon, I realized. Zeus would decide when we slept, when we were tired, what we would do.

When was the last time I'd slept? Had it been a couple days? I'd been moving from event to event and wanted to rub my eyes, but the helmet was in the way.

I thought about visualizing it opening. And right as I did so, a whirlwind almost knocked me over.

"Amira here. They dumped the air," Amira reported on the arm's channel. "Everyone helmeted? Call it in."

"I'm here."

Amira sounded annoyed. "Who the fuck is 'I'? I don't know your voice yet. Use your name."

"Sorry. Casimir here."

"Amabel."

"Roger."

"Katrin."

"Grayson."

"Devlin," I said.

"Haselda . . . shit," she grunted. "Just landed on my face. I'm here."

I looked around and saw a figure standing up from a divot in the dirt.

"Welcome back to the training area," Zeus said. "We have prepared an obstacle course for you. First arm to the other side gets dinner. The losing arms get to run back to this side and go hungry. Go!"

"What is their obsession with starving us?" Amira grumbled.

"Let's go," I grunted. "Let's just get this done."

We loped forward along the dirt trail leading to the other side. The first obstacle: a tall stone wall with barbed wire at the top.

"And up we go." Amira leapt nearly fifteen feet into the air, skimmed the barbed wire, and disappeared over the other side. "Careful, water pit on the other side," she reported.

I leapt. I didn't quite coordinate my jump, so I didn't reach the top. I struck the wall, stone broke and crumbled, and I flipped forward, landing in the pit of water upside down and flailing.

A suit landed nearby in an explosion of water, and the

helmeted head turned down to face me. Ken's voice came through on the public channel. "I *thought* that was you, Devlin. Graceful."

I struggled to stand, and Ken shoved past me, checking me easily with a shoulder. I toppled back into the water. "Damn it."

Ken leapt out, streaming water behind him. He hit the ground and flexed his knees, then jumped like a cricket to a spot another twenty feet away.

"Come on, Amira," I called out.

"Let it go," she said. "Haselda's having trouble getting over the wall."

"Casimir, help Haselda," I ordered. "Everyone else, keep up with me." Why was Amira arguing with me over the arm's channel? I was the octave. I was the leader.

I ran after Ken through more pits of mud and water, and then crawled quickly under crisscrossed lasers that sizzled against the suit.

The ghostly word OVERHEAT flashed in the lower right corner of my helmet's screen, some kind of heads-up display popping into my field of vision, but it faded as I crawled away.

I battled through a hell of competing wind and firestorms that buffeted me. Staggered through what looked like a pool of acid, took a running leap, and jumped out over a chasm.

I didn't realize how deep it was until the midpoint of my leap when I looked down, and 800 FEET appeared along with a range finder on the heads-up display.

"Shit." I wouldn't have jumped if I'd realized the fall could kill me.

I'd assumed the training grounds were a safe place. But they weren't. Maybe that acid would have eaten through my suit if I'd taken too long.

No one was playing games here. The Accordance wanted

to train us to fight an enemy they feared. They weren't holding back.

Zeus hadn't cared about Keiko. He didn't care about me.
We were aliens to the Arvani. Aliens they needed to train to
fight.

Disposable.

I slowed down. Took the obstacles more seriously.

Survive, I thought as I ran toward the wide maw leading
out of the crater training grounds. I wanted to survive this.

The remnants of other arms straggled in. My vague fan-
tasy of grabbing Ken in full armor and knocking him down
had faded. I was just glad Amira and I had struggled across
into the tunnel in one piece.

Zeus thudded across the metal floor. "Where is the rest of
your arm?"

"Behind us," I said.

"Unacceptable. Where is Haselda? Have you looked into
your arm's welfare? Have you kept it together and used it
effectively?"

I looked down at the ground. "No."

"Useless ape," Zeus hissed in my helmet. "You are an octave.
Act like it. Everyone, strip out of your armor, that's enough for
one day. Hart, you'll be outside running laps without the suit."

I started to work on cracking out of my suit as the rest
of my arm caught up. Again, visualizing the action sent the
command through whatever had slipped itself into my spine
and did the trick. The chest cracked open. Haselda limped in,
held up by Casimir.

The large doors leading out to the crater rolled shut. More
helmets snapped open and slid down into the suit collars. "Are
you okay?" I stopped focusing on trying to get out of my suit
and walked over. It resealed itself up the middle of my chest.

Blood ran down Haselda's lips from her nose. She walked past me, looking weary.

"Casimir?"

"She hit the wall headfirst after the first stumble," he said. "And then you left us behind. Nice work, man."

"You know what," I said, temper flaring. "I didn't ask to be an octave. I didn't even fucking ask to be sent here to the moon."

"Let's just get out of the power armor and take our medicine," Casimir said tiredly.

Amira moved in closer, her voice tight. She'd shucked her armor already. The neural interface was easy for her. "They're depending on you, Devlin. And we're going to have a lot of time stuck together."

"Hey!" Ken had his helmet flipped down and walked toward me. "You know what you are? You're a disgrace. You're a coward. You don't deserve the honor of being an octave, because you don't even want it."

It stung because it came too close to the truth, which I knew deep down, but on the surface I exploded. "Hey, asshole. Who ran from Tranquility when the bomb went off? You did. You left Keiko to die."

That hit home. Ken came at me swinging. I put up a gauntleted hand to block his punch, and then smacked into him just as hard.

"Guys!" Amira shouted.

We grappled and swung around. Then separated. "Asshole," I muttered. "You've been at this since the Hamptons. You need to back the fuck off."

"Go back home, traitor."

"Stop it!" Amira snapped, sounding utterly exasperated. She stepped between us, and I pushed her aside to get at Ken.

My forearm struck her with a loud crunch, and both Ken and I froze.

Amira didn't make a sound; she looked annoyed as she collapsed. Then she grabbed her stomach. Her eyes rolled back into her head.

"Amira, oh shit." I dropped to my knees. I was in power armor. Five times as strong. She'd stepped out of hers. "I'm sorry. I'm sorry. It was an accident."

"Step aside." A struthiform shoved past me. Another whipped in next to Amira. Medics.

"Is she okay?"

"Shut up," Zeus said. One of his mechanized tentacles grabbed the back of my armor and yanked me off my feet into the air.

Amira was rolled onto a stretcher, and the struthiforms picked her up and left the room. I struggled to get down and follow her, but Zeus held me up. "Careless," he said. "Useless. You're done. You are no longer octave. Get out of your armor, go outside. Start running. I'll come get you when you're done."

12

No one met my eyes as I walked down the rows of tables with my tray of Accordance human-optimized food. The gray goop and energy spheres wiggled with each step, and the square protein bars slid around the nonstick surface.

I tried to sit with my arm, but Casimir shook his head as I moved to swing my leg over the bench.

"Oh, come on," I snapped. I'd been isolated from everyone for an entire day; wasn't that punishment enough? "You'd all be licking Ken's boots right now if it weren't for me."

"Maybe," Casimir said. "But Amira wouldn't be laid out with crushed ribs, internal bleeding, and maybe worse."

"They said she was going to be okay," I said firmly. Accordance medical technology was near magical. Everything was okay.

Or, at least, I kept telling myself that.

Haselda sighed. "You've got to be kidding me. . . ."

Roger Li shook his head. "You need me to translate?" he asked sharply. "No one is happy with you here."

"This is high school shit," I snapped. "I made a mistake. **93**

I admit it. I fucked up, big. But I'm still part of this arm. I can sit at this table." In fact, I'd pulled this whole group together.

But that didn't mean jack, apparently. Grayson stood up and loomed over me. "Look: We'll train with you, yeah? You're part of this arm. But at this table, right now? You're not *fucking* welcome."

I picked up my tray with its wiggling, alien food, and moved on through the chatter of the mess hall. Faces I vaguely recognized glanced at me, then went back to conversing and eating.

The mess hall was on the rounded edge of the leaflike barrack building radiating out from its hub, the crater. A set of floor-to-ceiling windows looked out over the pitted and pocked lunar dark side. I sat by myself and gazed over the barren gray hills in the distance.

Something twinkled and flew out over the craters and hills, rising as it shot away over the lumpy horizon. A minute later, another twinkling sparkle flung itself out into the darkness. The mass driver over the hill was patiently slinging its pellets of raw material out into orbit, regular as a metronome.

As those pellets circled out from the dark side of the moon, they'd probably come out of the moon's shadow and into the light, and see Earth.

It had been only a couple days since I'd last seen it from Tranquility City, but for some reason time had stretched and everything that had happened there felt like it happened both an hour ago, and forever ago. Every time I thought about seeing Earth over the lunar hills, I felt the punch of an explosion, the rush of air leaving my lungs. Blood on my hands.

Shivering, I poked at an energy sphere until it broke apart and spilled liquid all over the tray.

+ + + +

A simple schedule started to form for us. The last two days we'd been run across the crater, herded, drilled, and yelled at by struthiforms, carapoids, and Arvani instructors in the morning. Or, at least, the first four hours that the lighting throughout the base was on.

In the "afternoon" we had an hour to eat and rest. Most snarfed their food, like I had, so they could use the time for themselves. After I tossed my tray, I straggled behind a small clump of recruits walking back to their bunks.

"Too fucking exhausted," a familiar American voice muttered in front of me: Amabel Lee, who sounded faintly like the acting president but without the creepy factor. "I'm just going to lie down on top of my blanket and die for a half hour. Wake me up?"

"I could wake you up," Casimir said with a tired sort of leering in his voice.

"Don't do that," Amabel said. "I'm too tired to tell if you're joking, flirting, or being creepy."

"My bad," Casimir said.

In the corner near a supply closet, two couples leaned against a crook in the wall and made out haphazardly. Casimir snapped a towel at them. "Asshole," the girl muttered.

We might be exhausted, on the dark side of the moon, monitored by aliens, but that wasn't going to stop human nature in any way, judging by the sounds late at night.

Casimir and Amabel walked into our bunk room. Our whole arm slept here, and there were eight rooms for the eight arms of this wing, housing all sixty-four recruits. After our class proved its worth, we'd been told, more humans would be pulled into the elite Darkside training program, and all four wings would be filled with recruits.

I looked in the room. The bunk near the door would have

been mine, as octave. Instead, Casimir flopped onto it and noticed me.

I nodded neutrally and kept walking past the door. I hadn't planned on lying in uncomfortable silence there, which was all I'd gotten the past two days whenever I was in the room.

The sickbay for this wing was right off the great doors leading into the training crater. The struthiform medics had turned me away each time I'd tried to visit, but this time they let me through.

"I'm here to see Amira Singh," I told the struthiform medic in an alcove by the door.

It looked up from manipulating three-dimensional images of some pink-and-purple alien anatomy. The large ostrichlike face had been reshaped in some horrific accident and then fixed. Parts of its face were artificial, and matte-black patches of machinery pocked the face where fine down should have been. Scars ran up and down the slender neck. "I don't know what an 'amirasing' is," it said.

The struthiform stood up, the thick left leg hissing at it did so. Synthetic. And the winglike hands, also heavily scarred, had some digits ending in prostheses. I took a step back.

"Amira. One of the recruits. That's her name."

It cocked its head, the scraggly feathers above the hard shell of its nose wafting about. The limpid eyes blinked. "I don't know your names."

"Well . . . why not?" I found myself asking, while also mentally slapping myself. Even by alien standards, this one seemed a little off.

"Names don't really matter, now. We are all just feed for the machine." It pointed claws at my chest. "I will fix you, I will tend to you. But I will not learn who you are, because I never wish to have known you. It will only be another emptiness pulled from me if I did that. I will reward you by not burdening you with my own method of self-identification. It is a gift. Say, 'thank you, medic.'"

"Thank you, medic," I stammered. "I guess I hadn't realized you all had names."

"Why, have you never asked one of us?"

"Usually you have your boots on the back of our necks."

The struthiform raised its wings. Shit. I was in trouble. But after a second of it tapping the floor, it lowered them. "Well said. They are so enthusiastic about doing Arvani bidding, aren't they?" It stomped the floor again. "We are scared. Every one of us you meet, that is the last of the clutch."

"What do you mean?"

Wing hands drooped and feathers ruffled. The struthiform sat back down at its station. "Arvani said I would soar the dark skies to protect my clutch. But instead I burned. But in this war, there is nowhere to go back to. Instead, they have pieced me back together and I'm alive once more. And before I burned, I saw my world fall to the Conglomeration. Without the brood nests and mothers, the Thunder Cliffs, the great Joins, there are no more clutches. Arvani tell us we will retake the home world. But, with each battle, it is farther and farther away, and more of us die. Do you think I will see the end of my species, human, or will I die before that happens?"

I stared at him. "I don't . . ."

"The one you seek is in the first room, a member of your arm. I would not go see her, though. There will be greater things to worry about soon, I imagine, and you must save your strength."

"I'd still like to go see her, though," I said.

"Then go." It waved a wing hand.

I hurried before it could change its mind and walked

quickly past shimmering energy curtains and spiderlike machines that hung from cables in the ceiling. Surgical robots that could, in seconds, pull you apart, fix you, reassemble you. Emergency medical pods lay in half-repose, shells open and ready to hug a body, whether carapoid, struthiform, human, or Arvani.

I stopped at the first door and glanced in. Amira lay back, ensconced in a medical pod. Tubes led out from it to plug into the wall.

She was sitting up and talking to Katrin, who loomed over her while Haselda sat on the edge of the pod nodding along. Amira's face looked puffy, and her right arm was purple with bruises. I winced.

Everyone stopped talking when Amira noticed me at the door. Haselda and Katrin looked at me, then back at Amira, looking for a cue.

Amira raised her right hand, and then made a dismissive wave. The door slid shut in front of me.

Message received.

"Heads down!" Casimir shouted as we huddled behind a pile of debris late the next morning. Now our octave, he radiated frustration. We'd been tasked with claiming a muddy pit up the hill that was currently occupied by Ken's arm.

It wasn't going well.

We didn't have real weapons yet. We just had training handguns and rifles.

"We have a full inventory of native-made weaponry," Zeus told us when they'd handed out the training weapons with human handgrips. They looked . . . close to what we expected a weapon to look like, but as if someone had melted them and stretched them. Accordance loved their smooth-flowing organic shapes. "We have native handguns, machine guns, submachine guns, and shotguns. But they all, primitively, use bullets. And we can't train with bullets, can we? Instead, you'll be using human-grip light trainers. One handgun model, one basic rifle with a variety of simulated fire rates. Even though these emulate Accordance weapons, you will be assigned native weaponry for battle. Accordance weapons are for Accordance fighters."

Our training weapons spit out a blue laser light with roughly the same power as a toy pointer you might use to drive a cat crazy.

But sensors all over our suits would shut down the power armor and freeze any part of the suit that got hit. Which was why Katrin was pulling herself up toward us without the use of her legs.

"Grayson, we need to flank them," Casimir said to us. A heavy wind kicked up, scouring us with debris and knocking some of us over.

"Someone needs to help Katrin in," I said.

"They're trying to lure us out," Casimir said. "Ken's arm chose to shoot her in the legs to draw us out."

I knew it was just a training mission, but seeing her slowly pulling herself toward us didn't feel right.

Something zinged overhead. I caught a glimpse of scaly, waving legs and a spiny pink tail.

"What was *that*?" Haselda asked.

Even though I'd only seen it out of the corner of my eye, I knew what it was. We'd had the lessons drilled into us so many times, I'd felt a chill down my back. "Driver," I said. "It was a driver."

"It can't be real," Haselda said.

"No more real than our pistols," Casimir said. "But . . ."

A driver bounded out of the slurry of wind and dirt, smacking into Katrin. "Shit," she grunted. "It's taking over my suit."

Despite myself, I relaxed. Katrin was alive and talking. This might feel real, but she was going to be . . . crap, she was on her feet and bearing down on us.

"Shoot her!" Casimir shouted, as if over the wind, despite the fact that we were all connected and listening via helmets.

I fumbled around and faced Katrin with my rifle. Then I shot her three times, nearly point-blank, as she jumped into our midst.

"Fuck!" She sprawled, perfectly still, between us all.

"I think they're trying to flank us," Amabel said suddenly. She was hunkered down just far enough away that I couldn't see her through the muck whirlwind.

"Where?"

We were clumped together, and vulnerable. Huddling. Waiting for Casimir to start acting instead of reacting.

And Ken's team would be able to pick us off easily in a few bursts of fire.

"I'll look," I said.

"Devlin, wait!" Casimir ordered.

I poked my head around the debris, not above it, flipping through types of imaging on my helmet to see if I could penetrate the artificial storm Zeus had whipped up for us.

Infrared. UV. Something that turned the entire helmet into black-and-white scratches. Was that radar? On thermal, something warm loped at us.

"There," I said, moving my rifle and firing. Once, twice. "Got it!" A driver bounced, lifeless, across the ground toward us.

"Dev!"

Something smacked into me from above the debris pile.

My suit lurched to standing, against my will. My visor went dark.

"Well done," Zeus said into my ear as I was yanked around to fire on my own team. "You've gotten yourself killed and become a walking corpse because neither you nor your arm covered an attack from the air."

It was all over in seconds. The storm faded away, and I regained control of my armor.

Zeus descended from the ceiling to point out to the other arms what we'd done wrong. Ken watched us, triumphant, from farther up the hill.

After we were dismissed, the arm trooped toward the racks by the bay doors leading into our barracks to shuck our armor.

Casimir got up in my face. "That was all on you, Hart," he hissed. "You shot us all."

I should have argued back, but for some reason I couldn't find the energy. Katrin was the first one to try to kill us in that exercise. And we shouldn't have all been huddled behind that rock pile together playing defense.

But I didn't say anything. I was just going to keep my head down and get through it.

In my sweaty grays I headed for lunch, stomach grumbling. This was all play, anyway. There was no blood leaking out of anyone into the dust. No real explosions.

It felt like we were playing on a distant, dreamy stage.

Amira sat at our arm's table. "You guys got your asses handed to you," she said with a half smile.

"Yeah," Casimir grumbled.

"Looks like you could use my help. So I'm back."

Our arm had its full strength back—Amira was okay to train.

The only good thing to happen so far today.

I leaned on the edge of the table, and no one said anything. I kept quiet, and listened to Amira and Casimir break down what had gone wrong.

"You should have kept your head down," Amira said coldly. "That's when it spotted you."

I smiled to myself, kept my face blank, and just nodded. She was talking to me again. That was a step in the right direction.

13

Three days. More drills. More drivers taking over suits and creating chaos within perfectly executed plans. Casimir stopped yelling at me after he ended up shooting us in the back when one landed on him.

A quiet peace developed between my arm and me. I kept my mouth shut, and they let me slowly ease my way back in.

We began to improve. Not as fast as the Arvani instructors wanted, though. Zeus and his two fellow instructors would stomp around the crater's obstacles in their armor to yell at any number of recruits. But by now we knew to sweep the air, the ground, and our perimeter. We could leapfrog our way forward and attack another arm.

Not bad, I thought.

"When do you think they'll give us the real weapons?" Haselda asked at one point. "Instead of the toys."

"We'll be playing laser tag until we stop getting our suits taken over by the mechanical training drivers," Amira said. "Right now toys are all we're ready for."

On the fourth day, all the arms gathered in front of Zeus.

"Four to eight arms," he declared, "make a fist." He pointed at us. "You on the left will be Red Fist. On the right, Yellow Fist."

We stood in the heart of the Yellow Fist.

We broke apart quickly, shepherded to either side of the crater on a run led by struthiform instructors.

"Your job is to take, and hold, the structure in the center of the training grounds." A ragged set of pylons and concrete had extruded itself from the ground. It looked somewhat like an ancient Greek ruin, but with alien curves and script on the broken columns.

"Who's in charge of the team?" someone asked over the general frequency.

"Fist," someone corrected.

"Whatever. Who's in charge?"

"Commander Zeus didn't say."

"We have four octaves; one of us will need to figure it out," Casimir's voice broke in. "Everyone else: Shut up."

There was a pause. Then, "I'm good with Casimir."

"Cas for me."

"The other fist is moving."

"Let's go!" Casimir ordered.

We bounded across the training ground, around caustic pits and mud-filled trenches, making the run back toward the center. It was exhilarating, until a bank of mist began to bubble out of the ground.

We slowed, suddenly unable to see more than a few feet in front of us. The edges of pylons loomed out of the murk at us. An acrid taste, like tear gas, briefly slipped through my suit's air before it switched over to internal recycling of air.

The common channel filled with a few coughs.

"I'm down!" someone cried out.

"Who said that?" Casimir asked, frustration in his voice.

And then the common channel erupted in chaos. Within minutes, Red Fist had taken a chunk out of us as we tried to organize.

Recruits lay scattered in unmoving suits, swearing and apologizing.

Instead of trying to hold the structure, Red Fist had run right through it to come out on our side and cut us in half.

"Now all we have to do is hunt you down and pick you off," said Ken over the common channel, glee in his voice. "Or do you want to just surrender now, Casimir, so we can all head in for lunch early?"

Commander Zeus interrupted, "There's no early lunch; you fight until I call an end to it."

"Casimir," I said on our arm's channel, working very hard to visualize sending the message correctly and not accidentally broadcasting to everyone. "If it's Ken, let me go out there and run around, create some chaos."

"That's a waste," Casimir replied.

"No. Ken hates me. He won't be paying attention if I'm running around shouting at him. Seriously, toss me out there, then counterattack."

Casimir was quiet for a while. I had almost never interrupted his plans, until now. Finally, grudgingly, he said, "Okay."

I leapt out from cover. I was good at sprinting, and the current gravity setting in the crater was comfortable. I ran and shouted on the common channel, "Ken: I'm coming for you!"

Flashes lit up the air around me: people shooting at me. But I ducked and weaved all over the debris at the center like an insane rabbit while shouting obscenities at Ken, wherever he was. Through rubble, underneath, around. I even managed to wing a few people with shots of my own, though after I got too turned around, I stopped shooting to avoid friendly fire.

Ken took the brunt of my shouting without saying a word, while I suggested what horrible things he did to squid-like aliens in return for their blessings.

I kept it up for a good five minutes until a suit struck me from the side and knocked the air clean out of me.

Ken's angry face stared at me, visor to visor. "You call me a tentacle licker one more time . . . ," he growled.

I did worse.

He punched my helmet with armored hands, while I laughed and lay in place. As long as he was focused on me . . .

The glass in my visor cracked slightly. "Hey," I said.

A spiderweb of cracks spread out with the next punch, and gas seeped in. I coughed. "Hey, you're breaking my helmet." I tried to struggle free, but Ken had me pinned, and another member of his fist had my legs.

He punched again, and now the acrid, yellow gas shoved its fingers in and filled my helmet. My eyes teared up, forcing me to close them. I gagged on the foul-tasting air.

"I can't breathe," I yelled. "Get the fuck off me. Get off."

Ken didn't say anything, kept punching, and glass shards hit my face as the visor completely broke. My nose ran, my throat screamed, I tried to hold my breath.

The next punch, I realized, would be to my face. With nothing to protect it, Ken might yet kill me. I rolled slightly over, jamming my face into mud and gas, and Ken continued hitting me, forcing my face down into it.

"That's enough," Zeus said over the common channel. "Red Fist has it."

+ + + +

By lunchtime the next day I had blown the last of the mud out of my nose, but still had the aftereffects of inhaling the gas. I'd spent the night in one of the medical pods, the cold biometallic arms wrapped around my chest as it monitored my lungs for any lasting damage.

Amira joined me to watch the twinkle of the mass driver's launches.

"You okay?" she asked.

"Not looking forward to running; still hurts a little to breathe. But they say I'm ready." I slurped one of the energy spheres. I was getting better at doing it without making a mess of myself. "I'm glad that half-cyborg struthiform wasn't on duty. Did you talk to him?"

"A cheerful one. He refused to tell me his name. It was his 'gift' to me."

"I think I'd be in even more of a foul mood if he'd talked to me while I was laid up there overnight," I said.

Amira laughed. I wasn't sure if the warmth spreading through me came from the drink, or because Amira put a hand on my shoulder. "We didn't win, but that was a smart move," she said.

She let go.

This was a possible reopening of our friendship. I felt relieved, like that simple touch had filled a massive emptiness.

"We keep getting matched up against Ken," Amira said. "You notice that?"

"They're pushing us."

"Zeus is. I had some time laid up in the medic bay to poke around. This isn't standard. Arms should be chosen by randomization for one-on-ones. Zeus keeps overriding. He's having fun with you two."

"Well, it's easy with Ken, isn't it? Just toss him into the situation—"

Amira interrupted. "Get real. You've been just as eager to needle him. What you did yesterday was tactically sound. But don't act like everyone didn't hear everything over the common channel."

I pulled back away from her. "Oh, you're taking *his* side here?"

"Damn it, Devlin, there are no *sides* here," she snapped at me. "There are only humans, who are not part of the Accordance. Who don't get to vote in Accordance affairs, or rise to be in charge. We are a client species. We are their cannon fodder. Ken knows it. You should know it. Spending all your energy worrying about him means you aren't paying attention to the real thorn in your side. So get your head out of your ass."

My ass? I opened my mouth to say something nasty back, and then closed it. Maybe I was tired from whatever they'd injected me with last night. Or maybe having my visor broken and staring a gauntleted punch in the eye changed something. But I bit my lip for once.

"At the very least," Amira said, "not being at each other's throats for the rest of training will make things calmer, yeah? And then he's out of your life, most likely."

Do the time. Get back.

I wasn't going to get back to Earth and my family if Ken punched my face inside out with power armor during a moment where Zeus couldn't stop him.

And besides, I didn't want to endanger Amira's goodwill. So I sighed and got up. "Okay."

I walked past the tables and across the mess hall. People glanced up, then realized my target. Conversation died down, more heads turned.

"Hey . . . ," I said, as earnestly as I could imagine. "Ken."

He turned around. His expression changed, lips tightening,

a controlled anger settling into his jaw. "Come to personally surrender before the next exercise?" he asked. "Get it all over with?"

"No." I thought about sitting next to him, but then thought better of it when I saw that the rest of his arm looked just as hostile. "I wanted to come and . . ." I realized how this looked. I looked weak. Fumbling over my words. Trying to apologize. Trying to patch things up. As everyone stared.

"Beg me to leave you alone?" Ken asked. "Put your hands together and get on your knees, ask pretty please?"

People laughed. I flushed. "You know what, I tried. Fuck you."

I'd tossed a match. I knew it. Ken knew it. He shot up.

"Look, let me take that back," I started to say, trying to fix the crumbling bridge. But Ken shoved me in the chest. I wobbled back on my feet, arms flailing. More laughter.

If I'd ever had any social capital in this room, it was all gone. "Stop pushing me," I hissed. "I'm trying to talk." I should have done this somewhere else, somewhere less public. Small gestures, leading up to a peace. Instead of this grand gesture.

"No one here cares what you have to say," Ken said, and stepped forward to push me again. "Go away."

I stopped his shove, blocking the movement and grabbing his hand.

He looked at me, then stepped right in. With a sudden ferocity, we'd locked. Grappling, we swung around twice, and then Ken threw me. I hit the table, smashing globs of food and bouncing off.

I launched myself forward and got one good hit. Right in the chin. Ken staggered back, and then we both exploded into an uncoordinated mess of punches and kicks, what little training we'd had forgotten as we tried to draw blood. Or at least a concussion.

An armored tentacle wrapped itself around my waist and picked me right off the ground, yanking me away from Ken.

Ken likewise hung two feet over the ground, his legs kicking wildly.

"You useless fucking apes," Zeus said. "You know, on our world Cal Riata like me used to find something shiny. Then we'd dangle it just out of the water by a riverbank until an ape like you would come down to the edge. Then we'd drag you under, drown you, and eat you. I can see the appeal."

I gasped, my waist squeezed so tight I could barely suck in half a breath.

"Let's fight," Zeus said enthusiastically. "This is what you do, right? Constantly war with each other? Squabble for the slightest reasons? It's in your nature. Between the fighting and your sexing each other every spare minute you have, it's a wonder any time is left over for training. So let's see it out."

Our nature? I coughed.

Zeus marched us out into the crater, through the rumbling bay doors, curious recruits following along to see what would happen.

But at a careful distance.

Zeus dropped us on a beam of metal above a frigid pool of water and shoved a stick in each of our hands. "There." He sounded satisfied, or maybe I imagined it. "Now you fight."

He left us shivering on either side of the beam and retreated to watch.

Was this standard? Was it a part of training to set two recruits to fight each other?

Ken moved across the beam toward me.

I kept the sticks in each hand down. "I'm not going to do this; this is crazy."

"Crazy because you know you're about to get your ass kicked."

I moved forward slowly. "This is what Zeus wants. A show."

Ken hit me in the stomach with one of the sticks. I doubled over, but didn't hit back. He frowned, and paused, watching me, waiting for a return strike.

"Hit him!" Zeus shouted, the voice echoing throughout the entire training ground.

Ken glanced over, struggling between wanting to obey the command and having to hit someone not fighting back.

"I'm done," I said. "I don't want to cause any trouble. I just want to focus on getting through this as best I can."

"Shut up!" Zeus ordered. "Listen up, apes, there's no talking on the beam. There's only battle."

Ken gave a halfhearted jab in my direction to see what would happen. I ignored it.

"I'm going to make whoever falls off that beam run around this entire forsaken moon," Zeus said. "With no food. Until you drop and beg for the chance to get back up here again."

Ken swallowed.

"Hit him!" Zeus repeated. "Or I'll extend the punishment to your entire arm as well."

Ken looked at me. "Fight."

"No." I shook my head.

"Asshole," Ken hissed, frustrated, and followed that up with a fast strike to my head.

I wasn't going to perform for the alien. I let the hit knock me off the beam. All the heat fled my body as I struck the water.

Enveloped by the cold, I slid down through the water, trailing blood. The cold made it easy to just lie back and let it happen.

I struck the bottom, fifteen feet below, in a state of calm.

Fuck this shit, I thought.

14

"Unfortunately," said a flat, toneless voice, "I recognize you. I apologize."

I tried to sit up with a gasp, but the familiar alien petals of a medical pod gripped my chest firmly. The struthiform with the burn scars stood in front of me.

"Should I tell you my name?" it asked. "Would that be fair? I know your name now: Devlinhart."

I swallowed. It hurt. Something had been shoved down my throat and pulled out. Maybe I'd inhaled some water? I remembered being yanked out by tentacles and thrown onto the mud by a disgusted Zeus.

"I'm Shriek, of the One Hundred and Fourth Thunder Clutch," the struthiform said. "What was it like?"

"What was what like?" I asked hoarsely.

"Dying," Shriek said conversationally.

I stared at him. "I don't understand."

"The Illustrious Leader, our Commander Zeus, left you in the mud without medical attention for a half hour, where you drowned due to inhalation of water when he yanked you out too quickly."

"The fuck?" I struggled to get out of the pod, suddenly feeling trapped and claustrophobic. The memory of water rushing up through my nostrils and gagging me filled the back of my head. "How long have I been here?"

"A few days. I had you sleep. Your arm is unable to visit; they are too tired. They've been made to run a great deal."

I groaned. "Zeus." If anything had thawed with the arm, it would be frozen again. They would hate me now.

"Far be it from me, a simple rebuilder of broken tissues and bones, a low-ranking survivor who failed to die defending my home, to criticize a great leader like Zeus"—the alien glanced down at a readout—"but such instructing might be considered by some, though it is not my place to say this, somewhat callous and wasteful of life. Luckily for you, I am here."

Shriek leaned forward and delicately tapped my nose with the tip of a finger claw. I jerked back and coughed.

"Yes, lucky for you," the struthiform mused. "And soon you'll be healthy enough to go back to training. And you, too, will be alive and full of vigor, ready to experience what it will be like to lose your own home world. Congratulations on not dying; the Arvani appreciate it."

I shook my head. "Lose our home world?" That didn't make any sense. "The Conglomeration is light-years away. That's why we're going to be shipped far off. Why our volunteers have yet to come back."

"They are light-years away. But what are light-years to beings like the Pcholem, who run the Accordance's starships? They live in the Great Ships, skipping from star to star. And for the Conglomeration, a light-year is a few months' journey. Look at my scars, human. They're closer than you think.

If they found you like we found you, from all the noise you broadcast out to the suns, it will not take them long to come sniffing around to see if your genetic stock will add value to the Conglomeration. I wonder what they will use humans for. I'm told my kind were rapidly evolved into package delivery systems." Shriek held up wing hands and looked at them. "I hear we can fly again now, even though free will has been bred out. I wonder if there is any joy in flying on your own."

Alarms wailed through the sickbay. Shriek snapped around and looked over at another pod. Someone flailed inside it, spitting blood as the head jerked back.

Shriek ran over, waving wing hands and pulling up holographic interfaces and controls. Another struthiform joined him. I watched as they moved furiously around. Aliens, and yet the flurry of doctors around a hurt patient an all too recognizable activity.

Then silence fell. A pale face slumped back in the pod as the machines all withdrew. I stared at the unmoving body on the table.

"Who was that?" I asked. "Who *was* that?"

"Don't ask that," Shriek told me. "You know you shouldn't ask."

Another struthiform checked my pod over, and then released me. I stood by the open bio-mechanical petals, looking over at the cluster of aliens around the limp human body.

"Go!" one of them ordered me firmly. "Now."

I cleared out of the sickbay, slowly walking back through a silent mess hall. The arms' bunks were empty. I found mine and lay down in it, shaken.

I hadn't achieved anything with Ken. I'd shoved the arm into even more trouble. Zeus had an eye on me. It was all a mess. And what for?

Just to survive? I'd watched someone die in a pod that had more medical technology in it than most of Earth had before the invasion. More medical tech than most people still on Earth had.

That shaved head had just lolled. A stranger, but maybe someone I could have met, or gotten to know, while training here.

Was it better to not know their names?

Because we're just cannon fodder for some upcoming clash of two alien civilizations?

I curled up into a ball and shivered. "Fuck."

There was no way out. There was no coming back. I'd been fooling myself. The only way out would be the same way I came, I thought. I remembered landing at the base. The lunar vehicles sitting in rows near where the elevator had stopped.

If I wanted out, I would have to get out.

I had to get ready to get out.

I sat up, looked around, and realized I had nothing to take with me. There was no "getting ready."

If I wanted to live, and not die in some alien war or right here in training, I needed to walk away now.

But going AWOL on the moon was going to be hard. And as soon as I got to Tranquility City I would have to get a message to my parents to run so they could survive, too.

The lunar rovers, blocky and ungainly on their oversize balloon tires, looked like silvered alien beetles on wheels sitting in pools of shadow. Instead of massive compound eyes, there were cab windows. And awkwardly jointed arms folded across their fronts were mechanisms that kept the passengers inside.

The rover nearest the bay airlock opened up when I tapped the door handle, swinging up over my head with a hiss. I jumped in and pulled it shut behind me.

"Okay, that's halfway there," I said aloud. In the cab, what was clearly a key hung from a hook near the dash of somewhat familiar physical controls.

There weren't a lot of vehicles for humans to operate; the industry had been taken over by the Accordance. But I'd been in a few. Seen enough shows. I felt I could run this.

They'd left the keys in the ignition, I thought. Idiots.

I checked to make sure they had human suits inside the locker by the door. I didn't want to make it all the way to Tranquility City, then get stuck because I couldn't sneak in through a quiet airlock.

There was a human-compatible suit in a baggie. I put my own bag of energy bars and liquid food bubbles next to it.

Back in the seat I started puzzling over the controls. I found the language swap screen and watched the panes of information around me reconfigure into English. Alien glyphs shifted into readable figures and icons.

And I would have to figure out how to trigger the vehicle airlock from here to get out onto the lunar surface.

Sitting still, poring over the read me files, I jumped in place when a fist smacked the glass right by my left thigh. "Shit!"

Amira stood in front of the rover, expression inscrutable.

Shit.

15

"You can't open the airlock yourself," Amira said, brushing past me. The rover door shut behind her and sealed with a soft clunk.

"I've got the help files up," I told her. "I'm figuring it out."

We sat down in the two cab chairs, looking out toward the vehicle lock.

"That was a statement, not a question," Amira said.

The entire rover jerked forward. "Got it," I muttered. Just a test, to see if I had it figured out. I could drive the damn thing now.

"The doors require an authorization code," Amira said. "Why do you think they left all the keys inside?"

Damn. "Wait, how do you know they left the keys in?"

"I snuck back here the first night. Took a look around. Always know your landscape. And your exits."

"But you didn't leave," I said.

"Not then."

I looked anywhere but at her. Thinking. Then I stabbed the controls forward. The rover lurched on, picking up speed.

"I watched a recruit die while I was in the sickbay," I told her. Knowing what I knew about Amira, about that nano-ink, if she'd been in here and there was a code, she knew it. "How many more are going to die? That struthiform, the scarred one: It calls itself Shriek? It told me about its dead home world. That the Accordance is slowly losing and falling back. And what are we going to get, for dying for them? Will they leave Earth, finally? Am I crazy for wanting to run?"

"I'm not going to open that door for you. You have no idea how stupid this idea is, do you?"

"I'm not going to slow us down. I know it's on manual now, so as long as I'm pushing these controls we're headed for that lock."

We stared at each other.

I continued, "If you're in the rover and we crash into the wall, you're going to have to come up with some kind of story."

Amira didn't reply. But the massive locks split apart, the gentle thrum of their separation accompanied by a steady rumble and the high-pitched whistle of escaping air.

I let go of the controls and we ground to a halt, half-in and half-out of the locks. The inner door was closing quickly behind us to prevent more air from getting out. I had been holding my breath. Amira was shaking her head.

"I'm masking everything. Including the damn loss-of-air indicators you just set off. By the time they notice what happened, we should have at least a day. You have food with you, water? Suits in the locker?"

"Yes to all three. Do you want to use a suit to get out?"

"No. Take us out."

I stared at her. "You're coming with me?"

"Without me you won't even make it out of the base's

perimeter without setting off every zone alarm out there. Come on, let's go."

Still unsure, I gently moved the rover the rest of the way out. The outer metal maw closed behind us.

My eyes adjusted to the vista of gray hills and pitted craters in the gloom of distant lights. I eased us out and away.

Amira muttered directions to me, guiding us around craters and the bases of hills as she used satellite data to map a course that wouldn't get us stuck somewhere.

"You did the right thing at Tranquility. I like that. But this? A very stupid idea," Amira said. "I just wanted to put that out there."

I'd been tense, waiting for something like that. "It's the only idea that guarantees we don't die in some pointless, far-off, alien war."

"It's a stupid idea for *you*. Your family will pay the ultimate price if you go AWOL here."

I flushed. "Maybe they should've thought about that before becoming terrorists."

"Oh, come on." Amira shook her head. "Even you don't believe that. Protestors, irritants, problem makers. Yeah. But your parents weren't setting off backpack nukes in downtown Atlanta to take out Accordance oversight buildings. And you're lucky to have them. Some of us aren't that lucky. But there are others who will pay a big price if you go all the way with this."

"Who's that?" We dipped into a crater and the tires kicked up dust. It hung in the air behind us for an eerily long time.

"Your arm, asshole. Zeus isn't quite right in the head as it is. What do you think happens to everyone after we're missing? Zeus may be an alien, but I can still spot a sadistic, disaffected shit who's abusing command easily enough."

"That's not an argument for me to go back. I'm done with it. I'm done with it all," I said grimly, looking out over the blasted lunar landscape. Now that we were ten minutes away I'd flicked on the lights. Driving near blind, depending on Amira's instructions and the instruments, had been a bit unnerving.

"It's a good thing I have a strong survival instinct," Amira said. "Because I wouldn't want to be back there when the shit hits the fan. You might toss them under the bus, but you're not taking me down with you. No one drags me down. No one."

A long stretch of flat lunar plain opened up in front of us. "Look," I started to say. But I didn't get to finish arguing about whether I was dragging her down or not. Amira slid out of her seat and jammed a baton up against my neck. "Hey!"

Lightning struck me. It leapt through my spine, up and down my ear, through my head, and out through my nose. I tasted ozone so deep in my sinuses, I breathed, spit, and coughed it.

My entire body spasmed, then seized. I tried to scream but managed only a gargle and fell over onto the floor.

Amira let me hit it, my head bouncing off the metal floor-boards. She squatted next to me as I struggled to breathe. Every cell inside me ached and protested. "I survived the Pacification, Devlin. I fought Accordance on the street. I helped lure their foot soldiers in to kill traps as a child. I kept people on the block out of their systems. I kept one step ahead of them for a long, long time. And now that's over. So understand me: I have no love for Accordance. But I can't have you fucking us all over, particularly me, because you had a bad few days and need to mope. Understood?"

I managed a moan.

"At the very least, I'm saving your ass. You know your

tattoo and rank, here on your arm, you know they have a transponder buried in them? It lights up on a ping; that's how I followed you. Wanted to make sure you didn't do anything stupid. Lucky me. But we have to head back before someone realizes you're missing. I can only delay and hide our little unauthorized lunar hike for so long."

She pulled out a couple zip ties. "What . . . ," I managed.

"For your own safety," she said, and zip-tied my arms to my legs. "Don't want you getting jumpy."

"Are you going to turn me in to Zeus?" I demanded sullenly.

Amira sat down and turned the rover around, heading right back for the camp. "As I said, he's a sadistic fuck. I wouldn't do that. But if we get discovered sneaking back in, I'll shove your zip-tied ass out in front of me as chum for that tentacled shark. Got it?"

I swallowed. "Got it."

16

I sat in a small bubble of my own angry silence. My wrists were starting to go numb, and even though Amira had taught me how to get out of them, while electrocuted and lying on the ground, I hadn't been able to move a single muscle.

My fingers hurt at this point. But I wasn't going to ask her for anything. And I particularly wasn't going to beg for my restraints to be loosened because I was uncomfortable.

The gray landscape, most of it shadowy in the dark because we'd killed the lights again, ghosted by the cab windows.

It felt like it was taking longer to get back. I leaned my head against the chair and closed my eyes, drifting off to the thump of the soft tires against lunar dirt.

"What was that?" Amira asked aloud, startling me out of my stupor.

"What?" Damn it. I spoke before remembering I was giving her the angry silent treatment.

She was looking through the upper cab windows. Up at the dark and stars. "Something . . . just grazed the sensors. Like an absence—"

Amira jerked back in her seat, her whole body taut with pain. At the same moment, the rover's interior lights flickered, then shut down. It coasted along on momentum, bouncing over a hole, and came to a stop. Amira grabbed her head and moaned.

"Amira?"

The sounds of fans circulating air faded away. An eerie quiet fell inside the rover.

"Amira?" I was a little freaked out. "Amira, what's wrong?"

We were busted. Fuck. We'd been caught, the rover disabled, and soon Zeus would come striding toward us. I was going to be deep in the shit any second now, and she was going to . . .

Blood streamed from Amira's nose. She rocked back and forth, mewling.

"Amira, are you okay?"

She pulled her hands away and looked at me. I gasped. Blood trickled out of the corners of her eyes, like red tears. "It hurts," she hissed.

"Can you see?"

Amira took a deep breath and wiped her bloody cheeks off with the backs of her wrists. "Yeah. Yeah, I can see. I lost some function, but I can see."

"What the fuck is going on?"

"Some kind of electromagnetic pulse. Anything non-hardened burned out. Some of my ink's military-grade; it's still running. Civilian stuff's mostly shot to shit."

I briefly imagined nano-ink sizzling all throughout her body, wrapped around nerve endings and skin as it bubbled and sparked. I shuddered and twisted my aching hands.

Amira saw the movement. She leaned halfheartedly forward and pulled a knife out of a hip pocket. After cutting me loose, she sort of hung there, holding the other seat and closing her eyes for a moment. "The air isn't being recycled," she said in a shaky voice. "It'll be okay for a while, but we need to check the suits. We'll use the rover's air until it's stale, and while I see if we can get a signal out, then switch to the suits."

I looked over her shoulder. "I don't think that's our biggest problem." This wasn't something Zeus was doing to us, I realized. Not punishment for stealing the rover. Not anything.

She turned. The lip of the crater above us glowed red, reflecting flashes of fiery heat. The horizon lit up, like lightning flickering away in a distant storm.

Then more red flashes danced out in the open, the hellish glow increasing. Balls of fire, dissipating quickly as the air vomited up into the sky, rising into the black night of the lunar dark before fading away.

"That's a lot of air lost to burn that long and high in the open vacuum," I said softly.

"It could be an industrial accident." Amira staggered to her feet. "The mass driver isn't too far away from the base."

"With an electromagnetic pulse? You *said* you sensed something in the sky."

She grabbed my shoulder and limped back toward the suits. "I *thought* I did. It could be anything."

"And the only way to know is to climb up and take a peek. How far away were we? Do you remember?"

Amira opened the locker and touched the nearest suit's collar. Lines throughout the suit glowed briefly yellow. "The suits are hardened, ready for a variety of outside jobs." She breathed with relief, resting her head against the locker's edge.

"There might be painkillers in the first aid kit," I said.

"No." Amira straightened with effort. "Might need it for later. Save it for when we know what's happening."

We pulled the shapeless suits on. Amira pointed out the controls on the left forearm's inner surface. Tap to make the materials tighten and shape to my body. Not too different from the backup manual controls for our fighting armor, really. But this one didn't slither into my back and link up to my thoughts.

"Don't use the common channel or speak while we're out there," Amira warned, before I tapped to make the helmet slide up out of the fabric and lock into place.

I nodded.

We bounded our way across the dust and up the side of the crater. The last hundred feet were steep: a rock climb, though falling would likely not be as dangerous as back on Earth. It was hard to figure out what a dangerous height would be, but we flirted with it.

I mostly worried about missing a handhold in the dark, and we weren't using any lights, even though the suits had built-in spotlights for just this sort of situation.

Huffing, I finally pulled myself up to the rim of ragged rock and looked out over the shadows and dirt between us and the conflagration.

The training base burned. The cap over the entire crater drooped, melting over what structure remained. Blackened spars jutted out in irregular directions.

Something moved above it. A charred, translucent jellyfish. It was massive. Almost as big as the base itself. We watched as bioluminescent light filled its interior, then traveled down through the long tentacles reaching the ground.

The behemoth's surface boiled with movement; not a single space remained still. Tiny sticklike insects fell away like dandruff, a cloud of brown that swooped around and clustered tighter as it dove into the ruins of the base.

I jumped as a hand grabbed my shoulder. "Hey," Amira said. "I'm patching a direct line via physical contact so we can talk."

"Those are crickets," I said. "Easily a hundred of them. This is a Conglomerate attack."

"Raptors are on the ground," she said, and pointed.

She was right. A dozen of them loped over boulders, clad in armor, kicking up dirt as they ran toward the base from where they'd been lowered by a tentacle away from the structures.

"Oh shit." Two rocky humanoid figures walked out from the interior of the Conglomerate ship. They leapt off from the edge of the gelatinous-looking rim, falling slowly at first, then speeding up. They struck the surface, throwing dirt up all around them and leaving small craters from the impact.

"Trolls." Amira's voice quavered, just as mine had.

The two creatures towered over the raptors at their feet as they stood and thudded their way toward the base.

17

More explosions ripped the base as we watched in horror. People we knew were trapped inside. People we knew were dying in there.

"They're switching to heavy jamming," Amira said. "Anticipating that there'd be a lot of hardened equipment around. I can't get the suit's comm systems to make contact with anything."

"So we have no idea if this is happening anywhere else? The moon, Earth, they could all be under attack and we have no idea?"

"We're in the dark," Amira said. And her hand squeezed my shoulder.

"Fuck."

"This isn't a large force, but I don't know what that means. It could mean they're just being detached to mop us up and all the action is elsewhere. Or it could be a sneak attack. And since we're on the other side of the moon, we can't even just wait to see if we spot any explosions on Earth to figure it out."

"We could run until we get out of jamming range," I said.

"And who knows how far that is? We have twenty-four hours of capacity in the suits. We probably blew out most of our air leaving the rover; it didn't have a proper airlock."

Another silent fireball rose above the base as something detonated inside. I flinched. Twenty-four hours of life left. My vision narrowed. What did that even mean?

The suit felt suddenly claustrophobic, my breathing loud and accusatory. Every breath, more air lost. Another lungful closer to a gasping death. "We're fucked," I said.

"We will be," Amira said. "We have twenty-four hours to think of something. To find air. Survive. The longer we keep going, the more options appear."

I looked out over the base, my heart pounding. This couldn't be happening. "For what? To die a few days later? To walk out across the moon and see Earth burning like Shriek said it would? I don't think I want to see that."

The image of an Earthrise came to me, but instead of a rich blue sphere I imagined the Earth burning as it appeared over the lifeless gray lunar surface.

"I'm going to choose life," Amira said. It sounded like her jaw was clenched. Fury filled my helmet as she continued. "Even if it's not for very long. I've fought too goddamned hard for every little scrap I've gotten. I'm not stopping now. I think we might be able to walk to the mines. I'm not sure if we can make it, but I'm betting there are supplies there, for the humans who service the automated launcher."

It was hard to hold two theories in my head at the same time, and try to figure out how to proceed while consulting both possibilities. One: The Earth and the rest of the moon were under attack. In that case, we were just buying time.

But if it wasn't widespread . . .

"Surely you can't attack an entire world without the

Accordance noticing *something*," I said. Two: only the moon was under attack.

"I was thinking that," Amira said. "Seems unlikely, doesn't it?"

"We need our armor," I said. "The rebreathers will give us enough time to walk out from under the jamming. Or at the least, get us to the mines for sure. How far away are they? Fifteen miles?" It had been hard to tell flying over. But I could see the launches from the base, so the launcher couldn't be too far away.

"Maybe."

"People can walk twenty or thirty miles a day, I think. But there are a lot of craters in the way to scramble through and around. I don't want to end up passing out a few hundred feet away from the entrance of a mine and dying there."

"Our armor is in the middle of a damn firefight," Amira said, pointing at the base.

"Yeah," I said.

"It doesn't look like they're taking prisoners from here. I'm not seeing anyone shooting back."

"We don't know what's going on, but we know the crickets are mostly patrolling, so it's a dozen raptors . . . "

"And two trolls."

"And two trolls." I nodded.

"They'll rip us apart if they see us," Amira said.

"Not if we can get to the armor first." I turned around and looked at her faint face behind the helmet glass. "I'll go while you wait, if you want."

"No. I think you're right. I can't tell for sure if we'd make the mines. It's a coin flip. But there's one thing still in our way." She pointed at the Conglomerate ship. "It'll see us. Any of those weapons it used on the base will make charcoal out of us."

Even as she said that, the organic structure wobbled. It glided out over the base and over toward the Arvani quarters.

"Now we have to run for the base," I said. "It's on the other side."

"Fuck," Amira swore. "Fuck. I know. You're right. I don't like it. Fuck."

I hid my relief. I knew I needed her abilities. Whatever was hopefully left of them. "Then let's do this," I said, with more confidence than I felt.

In the old history books my father had kept, I'd read with disbelief the stories of men in battle during a great world war. Huddling in trenches, they'd be ordered with a whistle to rush over the lip into horrible machine-gun fire and die in horrific numbers.

At the time I couldn't ever imagine anyone being able to move their muscles to stand up from safety and walk toward their own execution.

Yet here I was, moving down the outer slope of a crater toward the open plain between the base and us.

We used boulders and smaller craters for cover as best we could. But it was awkward to scrabble around in the lower gravity of the moon. We'd been mostly training in the artificial higher gravity of the base. It was hard to crawl on your elbows when a single shove could pop you back up to standing.

My helmet was filled with sweat by the time we scraped our way closer, waiting for the large Conglomerate jellyfish of a starship to rise up over the ruined top of the base.

But it was still busy on the other side.

Amira pointed at a large, still-glowing hole in the side of the base. I touched her shoulder. "Can you access anything?"

"Yes. Some of the cameras are able to talk to me, but I'm

low bandwidth. Mainly motion-sensing information, simple stuff."

"So is there anything moving on the other side of that hole?"

"Not unless it's waiting to jump us."

"Ah, shit."

"Better than standing out in the open," Amira said.

We didn't come this far to turn back. We bounced through the breach under the mess hall. I glanced up at the broken windows and saw a body slumped over. No head, just a bloody stump. Frozen blood made a long, ruddy icicle down the side of the black wall above us.

Gravity yanked at us as we stepped into the base. The plates below us were still working.

We skulked carefully around the corridors in silence, discovering more bodies. I didn't want to recognize the faces, and I was starting to understand Shriek's refusal to learn names as twinges of recognition lanced me.

Most of the faces I saw were gnarled into silent screams, struggles to breathe air that never came. Surprise. Fear. Unseeing eyes looking through me.

Long hair in a ponytail behind an emergency rebreather. For a second I wondered if she was passed out and lying down. Until I saw the horrible burn marks.

Some of the recruits had gotten to emergency gear, but then been shot by the Conglomeration.

Amira grabbed my forearm and turned me around. The doors leading out to the corridor had been ripped off. Plates bulged where they'd been forced aside.

"A troll came through here," she said.

The silver walls were covered in splotches of blood where bodies had been smashed against them and mauled.

18

I tapped Amira. "Wait."

I kicked at the yellow emergency box on the wall. Once, twice. The cover was warped, but remained closed.

"Come on!" I hissed to myself.

"Hold a second," Amira said, tapping my shoulder to make contact. "It's locked to recruits. Let me spoof the recognitions."

The warped cover twisted open as she waved a wrist over it, careful not to catch her suit on the sharp edges.

"Take the ax," she said.

"Sweet." I grabbed the ax inside. The handle, made for larger, alien hands, twisted and bulged awkwardly.

But it was a weapon, and holding it made me feel better.

Amira grabbed a can of fire suppressant.

We passed through the utility corridors in the subsections, walking right around clogged emergency airlocks and through gaping holes. Trolls, it seemed, liked punching *through* things. Several times we stepped over the bodies of dead struthiforms near reinforced bulkheads. They'd been waiting for the enemy to come at them through the doors.

Not through the solid walls.

It appeared the trolls had punched through the struthiforms as well. Alien blood saturated the walls and piles of organs lay on the floor.

We were going to have to pass the dorms to get to the armor. How many dead people were inside their rooms?

Amira slowed down ahead of me. I put my hand on her shoulder. "The sensors up ahead are down," she said. "I don't see any movement behind or ahead of the dead spot, though."

"Should I take a peek?" The emergency lighting faded away ahead. A pitch-black corner menaced us.

"My eyes are better," Amira said with gritted teeth. "You can't see in this."

She pushed my hand away and ever so slowly leaned around the corner.

Nothing happened.

I let out a deep breath. "Come on," she said.

We stepped around the corner into the dark. I lit up the corridor with the light on my shoulder, just in case anything dangerous was lurking there.

A crouched form cast a shadow on the gray floor. It turned a reptilian head toward us.

"Shit." Raptor.

The reddish armor jerked as the alien moved away from a body it had been inspecting on the ground and stood.

Amira shoved me back toward the corner, making contact for a second. "Run!"

I was already backpedaling as she passed me by, watching the raptor's long arms pull some kind of rifle up. The beady black eyes stared directly at me, cold and focused. I smacked the light off, plunging the corridor back into darkness, and

scrabbled around the corner as a line of pure, coherent energy struck the spot I'd been standing in just a split second before. *"Shit, shit, shit."*

The beam carved up the floor toward the corner, leaving molten metal behind it, until it struck the other side of the wall.

Safely on the other side, I spun around and ran after Amira.

Damn, she was fast. Left, right, I struggled to keep up with her turns. She was using a map in her head of the facility we'd already walked through and was moving us quickly back through it to try to shake the raptor.

But then she abruptly stopped and I stumbled into her. "This corner, make a stand," she gasped. At least she was also out of breath.

"We should run," I said.

"We can't. It's following us. It's catching up. I can't shake it. But I *can* see it. Get ready with the ax. We'll probably only get one chance."

How the fuck was she so calm?

I stood, my own heavy breathing filling the helmet, condensation trickling down it. If there were atmosphere, we would hear footsteps. But now I had to rely on Amira's vision of the raptor through the cameras.

"When I say 'swing,'" she said, "swing. Right at this height. Two feet out into the open corridor."

I shifted on my feet. This was happening. Now.

"Get ready. Three, two, one: Swing!"

Raptors, even in armor, stood only a foot higher than a human. I adjusted the ax and swung on pure faith as hard as I could. And at the end of the swing, the raptor turned the corner. The ax smacked into its faceplate.

It didn't shatter. Instead, the ax rebounded, hard. But the impact clotheslined the raptor, its feet flying out from underneath, and it landed hard on its back.

ZACHARY BROWN

Amira leapt forward and triggered the fire suppressant. She aimed it at the helmet, and gallons of foam covered the visor the moment she pressed the trigger.

I leapt forward with the ax and chopped at the raptor's helmet again. Foam and ax bounced away as we struggled.

The raptor got to its feet, us clinging to it. Amira dropped the fire can and went for the rifle the raptor was holding. The alien swung around, trying to shake her loose, so I climbed up onto its other arm.

Its vision was obscured from the foam, but it sensed the extra weight and started throwing elbows. The ax went flying, so I punched at its helmet: a useless gesture, but one I hoped at least alarmed the creature. I heard my suit rip as a claw grabbed at me, but I didn't have time to worry about it.

As Amira wrestled with the trigger guard, the rifle jerked up and around my head. I grabbed the barrel, shoving it toward where I though the raptor's chin might be, and my vision exploded with light.

We all three fell together.

My vision returned. There was no helmet anymore. Just a cauterized stump of neck where the armor stopped.

For a moment we lay on the alien's body, breathing hard, grateful to be alive. "We got lucky," Amira said.

"I'll take lucky." My hands shook. Each breath dizzied me. I'd been hit hard in the stomach, maybe broken a rib.

Amira fiddled with the rifle. "Shit. It's security tagged. It won't let me fire it. The rifle only fired because the raptor still had control of it when we were fighting. *Damn it.*"

I wasn't paying full attention. The dizzy feeling was all wrong. It wasn't from getting hit. "I'm losing air," I said, as I realized why the sensation felt so familiar. I remembered the ripping sound when the raptor's mechanical fingers had tried

136

to grab and break me as I wriggled and squirmed. "My suit's ripped."

I patted myself down, panicked, and found the long tear. The suit was trying to compensate by blowing air in for me to breathe as fast as it could. But that spiky, bruised feeling was my skin being exposed to vacuum.

I grabbed the ripped edges and pulled on them, then twisted them around until I could hold the rip somewhat shut.

Losing air still, but not nearly as badly.

The suit began a gentle beep near my ear. Low air warning.

"Quick," Amira said. She picked up the ax as we went past it and pulled me along with her other hand.

I staggered after her, my vision stuttering as I got to my feet. More lefts, more rights, as Amira guided us back through. I hesitated as we plunged into the dark again. And this time I didn't light it up. Let the monsters in the dark come for me. I didn't want to see them.

Amira stopped on the other side.

"We can't take the elevator or big stairs to get up above. Here's the emergency ladder." She lit up a shoulder light.

I stared at the orange ladder on the wall leading up to a hatch. "I only have one hand free."

"It's this or run into crickets. And I think there's a raptor coming down to check on its buddy who's gone mysteriously silent."

"I'm almost out of air."

"So move quickly."

I grabbed the nearest rung.

"Faster," Amira said.

I grunted my way up toward the hatch with little grace and a lot of swearing. "How do I open it?"

Amira was silent, her hand on my ankle. "Shit. Came down

with loss of pressure. There's air on the other side, but it doesn't want to open. Give me a second. Excuse me, hug the ladder."

She pulled herself up behind me, holding me against the ladder and looking up from my back at the hatch. I relaxed against her. I was getting dizzy, and I didn't have the energy to hold on. My hands were shaking, my legs close to giving out. The suit had switched to beeping insistently, and breathing was getting hard.

"Hey, you're getting heavy," she said.

"I'm sorry." I tried to pull myself forward.

Amira grabbed a latch and pumped it six times. "Okay, it's charged." She yanked it out, and the hatch popped open. "Fucking go!"

I launched myself through.

She closed the hatch behind us. I ripped my helmet off, flopped to my side, and took a deep breath of fresh, invigorating air.

Breathing. I would never take it for granted again. Such a basic, beautiful, primal thing.

"We can't stay here," Amira said. "There's movement. And we made a lot of noise. We have to keep out of their sight."

"I know," I said. "Just give me ten seconds to sit here and breathe. That's all I ask."

19

Inside the shadowy storage room Amira and I wasted no time struggling into our armor. She'd piloted us both around distant footsteps, the sounds of plasma fire, and screams to get us here in one piece.

"Never thought I'd be this happy to get back in this damn thing." I leaned into my splayed-open suit and smiled as it wrapped itself around me. I gritted my teeth as the suit wormed its way into my spine, but then relaxed as the neural interface synched up. I clenched a fist, feeling power surge through my forearms.

"Hold still," Amira said. "I'm disabling the training protocols. We don't want the suits locking up in a real fight."

"Shit." I hadn't even thought of that.

"Okay. You're good to go." Amira walked over to the door. Her helmet snapped up out of the collar ring and she held up a finger to silence me.

I snicked my helmet up with a thought.

"What's up?" I asked. With the helmet up, my voice wouldn't

carry. And with our quantum-encrypted comms, no one would be listening in.

"Gunfire. Hear it?"

Not with my own ears. And though I was interfaced with the suit, I wasn't quite as good as Amira at getting it to amplify things like that for me. That was going to be in the training ahead. Training we hadn't gotten to.

But then even I heard the crack, just down the corridor. "Quick, behind the open suits," I said. There were rows and rows of them on their wheeled racks, plugged in to base power and recharging.

Amira moved away from the door and joined me at the very back. We stood like statues in the ready position near several other broken, closed armor sets. I darkened my helmet. "We still don't have any weapons," Amira said.

"All we trained with were toys anyway," I replied. "We have the suits. That gives us a chance. More than we had when going up against them with an ax and no protection. Hopefully they won't even notice us."

The doors slid up, the light from the corridor outside spilling in. Two shadows darted inside. I could hear hushed whispers.

"They're human," Amira said with relief.

"I know." I slid my helmet down. The loud snicking sound made the shadows jump.

"Who's there?" someone hissed nervously.

I stepped forward with a thump, gauntleted hands raised. "Devlin Hart," I whispered.

Someone moved from my right. I hadn't even seen them detach and work around the row of suits. A flashlight blazed into life, and the end of a nasty-looking submachine gun jammed up near my cheek, making me wince.

"That's not a trainer," I muttered.

I turned and found myself face-to-face with Ken. He started laughing. "It's me, Ken Awojobi," he said, as if we hadn't seen each other in years. He grabbed the back of my neck and pulled our foreheads together. "You, you made it. Yes, you are too damn annoying and full of yourself not to. I love it. I am so happy to see you."

"You have real guns," I said, not sure how else to respond but to focus on the obvious. "How did you get them?"

Ken held up a hand and looked back at the door. "Everyone, in," he said with a wave.

More shadows slipped in, and one of them closed the doors. Once they were shut, someone flicked the lights on.

Amira shifted in her full armor behind Ken. He jumped away. "Fuck! How did you do that? I didn't even see you there."

She smiled. "How did you get the guns, Ken?"

Ken tapped the submachine gun. "You like my MP9? I've been waiting for us to go live fire. I wanted to see what our inventory was like, and one of my team members, Boris, was a recruit originally with the class in front of us. Held back for injuries. He knew where the good stuff was, and so did I. We went on a raid. Boris!"

"Incoming," Amira said.

A short recruit with a sharp chin joined our huddle. He held up a phone in one hand. "Raptor team," he confirmed with Amira. She nodded, agreeing.

Boris had a distinct South London accent. I imagined him loitering around an Accordance relief camp in the bombed-out ruins around the Thames, selling trinkets to struthiforms on leave.

Someone cut the lights, and we all tensed as raptors ran by outside.

"Okay," Boris said.

On some unspoken agreement, we didn't turn the lights back on. Amira lit her suit up, using blue shoulder lamps to create a soft pool of light around our sudden conference.

"How'd you get a pair of networked phones?" Amira asked.

"It's like lockdown back at home, isn't it?" Boris said. "Been playing keep-away with ET since I was yea high." He waved a hand near his waist.

"Boris gets you things," Ken said. "He had emergency air under his bed, in case Zeus tried something funny."

"Sadistic fucker," Boris said.

"We got more emergency breathers and hunkered down," Ken said. "Then the explosions and screaming started. We figured out it wasn't a drill."

"Shit went pear shaped," Boris put in. "So we snagged everyone with breathers willing to listen and made a dash for the weapons locker."

"A raptor jumped us on the way out." Ken rubbed his forehead. "It killed five of us before we put it down."

He wasn't bragging. Not trying to score points. He looked shaken mentioning the deaths.

"How many are near the door?" I asked.

"Outside of me and Boris, five others."

So just nine of us in the room. "Have you seen anyone else?"

"Just screams and bodies," Ken rasped. "Efua, you said you saw something?"

One of the other survivors had moved closer in the dark and spoke up. "We did see a cloud of crickets drag Commander Zeus off," she said. "We don't know what happened, though. Normally they don't take you alive . . . they just start firing first."

Commander Zeus must have had some value to them alive, I thought to myself. Unlike the recruits.

"I'd thought, once we had guns we could get armor and then fight back," Ken said softly. "But after that raptor . . . I realized we aren't ready for this. We barely started training. They're seasoned killers. After that encounter, I just wanted to get suited up and find a place to hole up. Fight only if cornered."

I nodded. "Amira and I were going to armor up, then go hide in the mines. See if we could get somewhere safe from there, or find out what's going on. Is it just here? Or is everything under attack?"

Ken looked up. "Like Earth?"

"The Conglomerate is here, and they usually come for whole systems," Amira said.

"Fucking hell," Boris said. "The mines aren't a bad idea."

"Can you really reach out from there to find out what's happening?" Ken asked.

"If anyone can, it's Amira. Anyone have a better idea to stay alive?"

Ken took a deep breath, then shook his head. He looked at Boris, who also shook his head.

Amira held up a hand. "Crickets," she said. "They're going door-to-door."

I turned to Ken. "Give Amira and me the MP9s you and Boris have, you all get into armor, and we'll hold them off."

Ken hesitated for a second, then handed me his submachine gun. He handed me an extra magazine. "Shoot sparingly, not a lot of magazines left. And we lost most of the other weapons in the fight. We just have some handguns passed around now."

Amira pointed at a rack of suits. "Ken, Boris, those suits are all the same arm. We're going to need to stay on the same network that they can't hack so we can chat. Everyone else, just make sure you're all in the same arm."

I stomped my way forward toward the doors and checked the MP9. "Is this the safety?"

Amira leaned forward and flicked up the switch I'd indicated. "Firing mode. Keep it off full automatic for now. Save ammo. The safety is in the trigger on this one. Just keep squeezing."

"Right." I didn't ask how she knew all this, but raised the gun and flipped my helmet up as the sound of skittering outside got louder.

20

The doors jerked up, a slight gap of light appearing before they seized. Amira had her eyes closed, concentrating as she fought to keep the doors from opening. Electrical smoke from burning motors in the doors wafted around us.

A pair of sticklike pincers reached under the door, trying to pull it up.

I stomped them, snapping the limbs clean off.

It was like kicking a beehive. Suddenly the entire gap filled with metal lobster-sized bodies thrashing to get through the gap and into the room.

"They know we're here," Amira grunted.

I aimed the machine gun low and fired along the floor. Pieces of cricket flew off and clattered to the floor with each shot.

"Save the ammo for something bigger!" Ken shouted from the back of the room.

I kept stomping. The door lurched farther open. I grabbed a cricket out of the air with my right hand and slapped it into a wall. It burst into parts and rained to the floor. One of the legs twitched and tried to jam a knifelike tip down into my ankle. I leapt back away and shot it.

Crickets zoomed around the room, bursting past us, seeking to stab anything they could. But everyone had armored up.

Cricket bodies were slammed against walls, pulverized under boots, or just thrown aside as we spilled out into the corridor. "Amira?" I shouted.

"This way."

We retreated from the swarm of metal insects falling over themselves to get at us. I followed Amira, crushing crickets underfoot. How far away was the breach that would get us outside onto the lunar surface? Because then we could really open up and run.

"Stop!" Amira shouted. "Raptors. Backup is coming."

"How many?" Ken asked.

"Four."

No way could we face four raptors.

"Back the way we came," Ken said.

"But . . . ," someone objected.

"He's right!" I shouted. "Come on."

We charged into the boiling mess of crickets, flailing and destroying as many as we could as we ran on. We skidded to a halt at another junction. Amira raised a hand.

More crickets scuttled toward us, some of them bouncing off the walls with eagerness. Why were we stopped?

Then I felt it: a thud in the floor under my boots.

"Troll?" I asked.

Amira turned toward me. Through the helmet I could see her face had gone pale. She nodded.

146   "Raptors to the back, troll ahead," I said out loud.

"I told you we should have gotten those fucking explosives," Boris said. "Take them with us."

I leaned against the wall, feeling each vibration of the troll approaching us. "We can't get to the breach," Amira said. "We're going to have to see if we can outrun them on the training grounds, it's the only direction left."

"That's something." I started backing down that corridor.

"It's just buying time," she said.

"You told me time gives us options." I was thinking.

"Troll or raptor, not much of an option."

"No, but we have something they're not expecting," I said.

"What's that?"

"*You*. The facility is still powering up the variable gravity. Can you access it?"

"I think so," Amira said. "You want me to use the field against them?"

"Captain Calamari did it against us. Should be just as annoying, don't you think?"

Amira started to jog faster. "Yeah. Yeah. I don't know how long it will take, though. Ken, take this MP9."

"We're going deeper into the base," I called out. "Cover Amira as best you can, give her space. If you want to get out of here alive, you'll make sure nothing touches her."

We burst out of the bay leading onto the center grounds and scattered without thinking. We'd been doing drills on the training field enough that it was instinct.

Only this time it wasn't a fellow squad coming at us, but real Conglomerate enemies.

"Keep moving," I said. "We have to buy Amira time."

"This better work," Ken grumbled.

Crickets tumbled out after us, some of them unfolding translucent wings and taking to the air. Then came the loping raptors.

I circled around the rim of a crater to get something between us as long lances of focused energy stabbed at us from the raptor's rifles, exploding dirt whenever they hit the ground.

Gunfire answered them. Ken perched on the lip of a boulder, sniping at them. He'd pulled the gun's shoulder stock out and unfolded the forward grip for better aim. The aliens scattered as well, hunting for cover as more accurate fire struck them.

The cap over the grounds had been punctured and melted, so there was no atmosphere. But Amira stood behind us and raised her gauntleted hands. "I'm into the training system's weather control. I think this will only hit them," she muttered to us. "But just in case, hunker down."

Fist-sized hail flung itself out of the sky on the other half of the course. Crickets circling overhead fell, wings suddenly punctured. The raptors huddled, distracted by the pelting chaos.

Without eyes in the sky, with the raptors knocked back, we took the chance to rearrange ourselves, finding the best spots on the course. Spots well-known to us.

One of the raptors broke cover and jumped into the air, looking for us. Amira waved a hand and the raptor twisted. It came right back down to the ground, faster than it had anticipated. It struggled to get to its feet, fighting the suddenly heavy gravity.

Ken fired three quick bursts at it. It reeled back and fell over a ledge, then slid down into the middle of a crater.

"One less raptor to worry about," he said.

But none of us were paying attention. We were all looking

at the rocky creature stooping out from under the bay door and stepping into our arena.

The troll seemed to keep unfolding, getting taller and taller. It took slow, deliberate steps forward.

"I've got gravity cranked all the way up," Amira said. "Overrides and all."

"Can you imagine the world that thing came from?" Ken whispered, somewhat awed.

I didn't want to.

"Anyone see something behind the troll?" Amira asked. "There's something there, right?" Her voice sounded strained. She staggered and fell back. I moved closer to her, leaving cover.

"Amira, what's wrong?" I moved around to look into her visor. She glanced over at me, and I saw blood run down her upper lip. Like it had when the electromagnetic pulse fried the computer chips and her unhardened nano-ink. "Shit. Amira!"

"Look at the troll!" she snapped. "Do you see something near it? I can feel it, all over the network. It's attacking me."

I looked again. Yes, something: a blur moving alongside the legs.

"Yeah. I thought something was in my eye, or on the helmet," Boris said.

"Ghost," Amira said softly. "It's a ghost." Almost too soft to hear.

"Fuck," I said. That's all we needed, the alien that caused all the other aliens to go berserker.

Amira's voice firmed up. "I think I can still work around it. It's everywhere, but I can . . . here we go, get ready to run."

Yellow mists rose from the ground. They swirled around the troll and the raptors and rose quickly. Other gases mixed in, and the entire dome thickened with them.

"Smoke screen. And they're slowed down. Now we run," Amira said.

Ken and Boris hung back to cover us as we bounced to the other side. A big leap with our assisted legs got us onto the scaffolding twenty feet over the grounds. Some awkward climbing and we broke out of the facility.

Another great leap for us, and we were on the lunar surface, bounding for safety in the shadows of the jagged hills and craters around the base.

"Faster!" I shouted at everyone. Over by the Arvani quarters the Conglomerate starship was pulling up its tendrils with surprising swiftness for something its size. Whatever it was.

It began to drift our way.

"I think it's coming for us," I said, just before thick beams of energy lit up the lunar night like searching spotlights, dancing around the battered gray rocks we were trying to hide behind.

21

The barrage melted lunar regolith and threw boulders into the air as rock exploded. Stabbing energy blasts dazzled my eyes as I scrambled for cover.

"They're climbing higher for an angle on us," Ken shouted after a few minutes of chaos and hell.

Someone started whimpering on the arm's channel. I sympathized as I huddled down into the shadows of a niche in a crater. "Stay still," Amira said. "The suits have adaptive camo. They have countermeasures built in for Conglomerate sensors. Heat, UV, color, EM. Just don't move, and the suit has the capacity to hide us. Move and it can't keep up."

I was already gray as the rock around me.

"Everyone should call in," Amira continued in a calming voice. "Who made it out? We didn't have time for names back inside. Who's in our arm?"

"Boris, me, you, and Efua are one arm," Ken said. "The other four are another arm."

If we used the common channel, the Conglomerate would

use the radio chatter to find us. The quantum entanglement only worked for intra-arm communication.

"Which one of us is closest to someone in the other arm?" Amira asked. "Are they moving around?"

"I am," said a voice that wasn't Boris's recognizable accent, Amira, or Ken's deep voice. She recognized the need to identify herself. "Efua here. I'm ten feet away from someone in the other arm. I don't know the person's name, but whoever it is saw us all stop moving and hide, and is copying us."

Good. I hadn't even thought about comm issues. If we'd been supported by properly trained octaves we'd know how to pass communications through from arm to arm, as well as ways to pass information up to leaders.

But we had no idea what we were doing. Amira was our most competent technologist, and she'd been hit by the electromagnetic pulse.

"Efua, can you safely get to this person and touch their armor?" Amira asked. "That'll set up a direct comm link, and you don't have to do anything. The suit should figure it out for you."

"I think so." Efua was silent for a long moment. "I'm going over."

We waited for her to do that. I winced as more energy struck the dirt nearby. But it was random fire.

"Where is everyone?" I asked after a few minutes. I hadn't been paying attention as we'd run for it. I'd dived into a crater a couple hundred feet away from the base. Ken was close to the bottom of the same crater, behind a boulder that had rolled down the slope. I didn't know where anyone else was.

"A little farther ahead on the other side of the ridge," Amira said. "I saw Devlin dive in. I risked the fire to get more distance."

"I'm right next to Devlin," Ken said flatly.

"Um . . ." Boris cleared his throat. "I'm near the rover bay, hiding behind one of the transport shuttles."

"You doubled back to the base and moved around to the bay?" Ken asked, beating me by a split second.

"Well," Boris said, "flying out with a shuttle when they're distracted might be easier than trying to leg it out, yeah? Also, I thought there might be some useful bits lying around."

"And?"

"I found a welding torch," Boris said. There was a faint hint of satisfaction in his voice. "It's supposedly strong enough to go through walls. I think it might go through raptor armor."

"Anything else useful?" Ken asked.

"Explosives," Boris added.

"Where'd you find those?"

"Locked away somewhere I had to use the torch to get at," Boris said.

"You could have blown yourself up," Ken snapped.

Boris made a noncommittal sound.

"We're all in danger," Amira said. "It's as good an idea as any. He may yet be the one that makes it out now that the damn ship is trying to melt us into the surface."

Efua interrupted us. "Okay, I have contact with the other arm. Is there anything you would like me to say to them for you?"

"Stay put," Ken said. "Tell them about the camouflage, okay?"

"Okay. I am telling them."

The light show stopped. The ground stopped shaking underneath us.

"What's happening now?" I asked.

"Want to take a look over the edge?" Ken asked. I couldn't

tell if he was being sarcastic or not. But someone was going to have to.

"Give me a second," I told him.

"Wait . . ."

I did it slowly, trying to give the suit time to adjust to the change. Hopefully anyone looking at this tiny little space at the crater's lip would see nothing but gray.

"Devlin, what are you doing?"

I tensed, waiting for a bolt of energy to smack into my helmet and take the top of my head clean off. Nothing happened. I kept moving until I finally peered over the edge of the crater.

I stared at the lumpy, bell-shaped head of a troll standing tall farther down the slope of the crater. "Oh shit."

It leapt into the air, passing over me and sailing into the center of the crater.

Ken rolled away from the boulder and started firing at it. The gun silently puffed smoke in the vacuum out of the barrel, and bullets chipped away at the troll's bulky ankles.

"Ken! Run!" Amira bounced onto the tip of the crater. She must have leapt as hard as the suit possibly could, maybe even killing overrides for safety, to make it back from the ridge in a single bound like that.

The large rock she'd been carrying continued on as she smacked into the ground. It struck the troll right in the temple, and the alien swung to look at her.

Ken leapt out of the crater. So did I. But Ken shot at the troll again, clipping it in the head, getting its attention back on us and away from Amira.

"Those bullets aren't doing shit!" I yelled. "They're good for crickets, that's it. We're just pissing it off."

"I know." Ken popped up like a tick, bouncing from boulder

to boulder, zigzagging and staying well away from the troll. "Efua, get your arm to the mining facility while we have the troll's attention!"

The troll stopped trying to catch him and pulled out a large weapon strapped to its back. More cannon than gun. Well, more sawed-off cannon than cannon, really. It was squat and oddly bulky. In fact, it was wider than it was long. A weapon that was almost all mouth.

"Cover!" I yelled. The cannon glowed white and blue, then spat a long line of darkness. Light bent and wobbled around it. The boulder Ken hid behind was plucked right off the ground.

"What the . . ."

Ken swore as he watched the large chunk of rock sucked toward the troll in a cloud of fine gray dirt.

I opened fire. "Jump away, Ken!" I shouted.

Bullets struck the cannon, knocking it sideways just enough that the line of darkness wobbled off to the right. With the cannon beam's hold on it broken, the boulder dropped, and Ken made like a grasshopper, shooting off for the ridge Amira had come from.

"What the hell was that?" he asked.

"I think it's packing something like a portable wormhole in there. A weaponized tractor beam," Amira said. "Ken, keep coming for the ridge, there are places to hide on the other side."

I leapt the other way, heading back for the craters. The troll bounded after me. Every time I landed, I spun off in a new direction, waiting for the line of darkness to reach out and grab me. Or for a giant rocky foot to plaster me against the surface.

I was rabbiting away, swerving this way and that as best I could, but it was slowly, ploddingly, getting closer. It had thrown the wormhole cannon away. Had I broken it?

"Hold on," Boris said. "I think I can distract it a second."

I turned my head back in midleap and saw the sparkle of an explosion in the bay doors. The troll paused the next time it landed, and then turned back for a second.

That's all I needed.

I skimmed low across the landscape and made it over a nearby set of ridges. Once I had lunar mass between me and the troll, I randomly bounced this way and that from hard, rocky surfaces so I didn't leave footprints.

And then I dug in and froze.

No looking over the lip and getting spotted *this* time. The troll was out there stomping on bugs, and I was going to be a good little cockroach and stay put in the dark crevice I'd found.

"Dev?" Amira whispered, even though she didn't need to. "You there?"

"Yeah. Ken?"

"Yeah. Boris?"

No reply.

"Boris?"

A loud grunt, some spitting sounds, and a metallic screech filled our ears. "Boris!" we all shouted.

"I'm still here," Boris panted.

"You okay?"

"I'm happy to report that the welding torch does cut through raptor armor," he said. "However, the downside is a bit limiting: You have to get rather close to them. Hang on."

The silence stretched. And none of us seemed to want to jinx it by saying anything.

Then Boris was back. "I'm sorry, I have to blow something else up."

A very distinct thump came through my helmet.

Amira swore.

"What's wrong?" I asked.

"The other troll just jumped past us, headed toward the mines. I think they spotted some movement."

"Efua?" I called. "Did you hear that?"

She didn't respond.

"There are," Boris interjected, "a bloody shitload of crickets swarming out of here. I'd stay very, very still for a long while."

"Are you going to be okay?" I asked him.

"I think I convinced them I blew myself up. I found a nice hiding spot in the wreckage; they're not pawing through it. So let's just wait for everything to die down, shall we?"

"Sounds like a plan." I was on my back, shoved deep into a crack. I stared at the rock above my helmet.

I'm a shadow, I told the lunar landscape. A shadow in the dark under this rock. A shadow that wasn't going to move for a good long time.

But that wasn't good. I had stopped running. Stopped moving around. Stopped reacting.

I had time to think now.

Time to think about all the recruits' faces that I'd seen mangled and staring past me as I passed them in the airless corridors.

Time to realize that Casimir wasn't going to ever bark orders at me. Katrin wasn't going to give me a disgusted look for breaking Amira's ribs due to my stupidity.

Right now, I'd trade anything for their frosty silence at the table.

I suddenly wish I'd never known their names.

And then I felt horrible for wishing it. I closed my eyes and began to shiver, hoping it wasn't causing my armor to twitch.

"Dig in!" Ken shouted.

The explosions started again. The Conglomerate ship, apparently not wanting to wait for the trolls to dig up every rock and crevice, floated over the landscape. A full-on barrage of furious light and energy danced around us. Rocks jumped and tumbled around me. New craters spewed liquified moon rock up into the dark, where it slowly misted and settled back down to the ground.

22

"You know what I've always wondered?" Boris suddenly broke the silence.

I snapped my eyes open and looked around. The crater was empty. I'd nodded off. I'd needed it. I glanced at the time stamp floating over the visor. I'd been asleep for twenty minutes.

Damn. I could have been killed in my sleep. Melted by one of those explosions from the ship.

"I've always wanted to know what struthiforms think of breakfast burritos," Boris continued.

"What?" Amira's voice sounded crusty and strained.

"It's the eggs, yeah?" Boris sniffed. "I mean, scrambled eggs. They're giant ostriches, how does that look?"

"Well, like us eating a small mammal, like a pig," Ken chimed in.

"Veal," Amira said. "Baby mammal."

"Hmmm . . ." Boris sounded unsure. "I guess so."

I opened my mouth to tell them about Shriek, and that the struthiforms were all dying because they couldn't go back to their home world.

But since we didn't know whether we were about to lose ours, why harsh everyone's mellow? "What does it look like out there? They still hunting us?"

Quiet.

"Hello, can you guys hear me?"

"Devlin"—Amira sounded worried—"what have you been doing the last half hour? Sleeping? We've been calling for you."

"Well . . ." I cleared my throat. "Yes, sorry. I nodded off." The regular rhythm of the bombing had become constant. A background noise.

"Damn," Boris said. "You're all ice. You slept through all that? Shit, I'm still vibrating."

I opened my mouth to reply. To tell them I was so exhausted, I couldn't help it, and that thinking about the dead just on the other side of the ridge was too much.

"They left," Ken reported. "Ten minutes and nothing has moved near me or Amira. No more explosions. No hunting parties."

"Could be a trap," Amira said. "We've been discussing that. Then Boris changed the subject."

"You were all boring me," Boris said. "I'm hiding under shuttle debris, and I can't so much as twitch, and you two are just going around and around. Not discussing. Arguing."

I looked around the crater I'd hidden inside. Nothing.

The debate started up again, Amira assuming that there were at least crickets out hiding away, as still as we were, waiting to get triggered. Ken insisting that he could move around his hiding spot.

I tumbled out onto the dirt and rock. I didn't want to put anyone else at risk, and we couldn't wait here forever. Eventually, someone had to be the first to put themselves in the crosshairs. If there were any.

My joints protested, but after a few seconds of movement, they warmed and loosened up. It felt good to stand.

Nothing moved but me. The attack I'd been half tensing for didn't come.

I scrabbled up to the rim and bounced off across to the ridge. "I'm out in the open," I reported. "Nothing coming after me."

"Shit," Ken said. "I knew it. I'm—"

"Why don't you two stay where you are," I interrupted. "Boris, you too. In case the enemy is waiting for more movement."

"Okay," they muttered.

I slithered up the rim and looked out over toward the Conglomerate ship. It hung over the main base again, tentacles down. There was nothing out on the plain between us but newly pockmarked ground.

"Did Efua make it to the mines?" I asked.

"We are here," Efua said. "We found some air canisters. We think. We're trying to understand how to hook them up to our suits."

"Can you call out from there?"

"No," Efua said. "We are still being jammed."

I looked at the ruins of the base, thinking. "Efua, you said the crickets came and took Commander Zeus away. To the officers' quarters?"

Efua was quiet for a second. "I think so. In that direction, at least."

Amira jumped in. "Zeus's transponder is there. Whether that means Zeus is there or not, I can't say. I'd need to get closer to verify, grab some higher bandwidth, line-of-sight comms."

"What about our rank transponders?" I asked quickly,

thinking back to Amira's lecture that the tattoos had trackers in them.

"I, obviously, killed them a long time ago," Amira said, almost as if she were talking to a child. "Or we'd be toothpaste under troll toes."

Sure. That made sense.

"What are you thinking?" Ken asked.

I looked off in the direction of the launcher. Safety. For now. What would a fighter do here? Hide like a cockroach? Until his air ran out?

Or . . .

Or what?

"Zeus and the other Arvani in their quarters, and the struthiforms, if they're alive, have heavier armor. They're trained for this. They're officers. They know what our options are. They've fought the Conglomerate before. We're untrained recruits. I think we need Zeus back."

"That sadistic bastard?" Ken asked.

"Captain Calamari is crazy," Amira agreed. "But Devlin has a point: We could aim that crazy at the Conglomerate bastards."

Boris laughed. "Captain Calamari? Why didn't I think of that? You even demoted him . . . to an appetizer! We called him Sergeant Suckers. I do have some leftover explosives for getting inside the Arvani quarters."

"Or we can just get me close enough that I can pop the locks. What are you thinking, Devlin?" Amira asked.

"We take our time. Shadow to shadow. Total sneak mode. If it feels risky, don't move. We have our suits, and we have all day to get there. We're going to converge on it from all points. No rush." We were going to be good little stealthy cockroaches. "If we get spotted, scatter and hide again. Once inside, kill anything in our way, get the commander and any other Accordance survivors."

"I like it," Ken said. "We take the fight back to them."

"And what about us?" Efua asked.

"Give us twenty-five hours from now. If we go silent, try to get out from the jamming and get a signal back to Tranquility."

"Good luck," Efua said.

"You too," I replied, and began to slither to the nearest rock.

23

Five hours. Five hours of slinking across the fields of gray waste. Five hours of waiting to get caught. Five hours of tension building. The closer we got to the Arvani officers' quarters, the more I felt like something in the back of my neck was going to snap.

"Worse game of red light, green light ever," Amira said.

One of us would advance, the other watch from a safe position, and the other two would stay hidden.

Foot by foot.

Inch by inch.

We converged on the airlock. Boris bounded up the last few feet, unslinging an arm-sized black claw with four sharp points at the end. The alien welding torch.

"We ready?" I asked.

Boris held up a disk. "I have explosives," he said happily. Then he awkwardly held up the welding torch.

Amira walked up to the doors. "I already said there's no need."

"We'll see." Boris strapped the disk back onto his hip.

Ken stepped forward. "Boris, you and me are in first, we have the guns. Amira, Devlin, come in behind us. Amira: when you're ready."

I got in place behind Ken.

"On three. One, two, three." Amira waved a hand and the airlock doors slid up and open. A cloud of wet air puffed out past us.

We slipped in, the outer door closed behind us, and Amira held up a hand. "There's a raptor on the other side," she said. "Wait a second. He's turning away. And . . . Get ready."

This was it.

I crouched. Ken pulled the MP9 up tight to his shoulder and Boris held up the torch. The four claw points lit up and glowed white-hot. Energy leapt out from each point and met in the air a foot ahead.

"Anytime," Boris said.

"Now." Amira waved her hand and the inner door opened.

Ken jumped into the air. The raptor spun at us, raising a weapon even as Ken arced toward it, firing with quick bursts that did little more than plink off the armor around the raptor's claws. The shielding was too tough.

But Ken had known that going in. He wasn't trying to break the armor. The kinetic energy of each bullet was hitting the raptor's weapon, making it hard to bring the burst of energy to bear on us.

And to give Boris time to close the distance without being carved up.

When Boris struck the raptor, both bodies tumbled end over end. And then he jammed the welding torch up into the raptor's jaw.

The white-hot energy point at the torch's end sizzled and spat as it ate right through the alien's helmet. The inside of the visor filled with steam and heat, then burst open like wet fruit.

Boris shoved the armored corpse off and to the side, jumping up, ready for the next attack.

Nothing.

We stood on metal grating that led down to a very tropical-looking spit of sand, and beyond that a deep pool. Purple-and-black shrubs cluttered around in transparent tubs, their fronds dropping toward the water.

In other rooms leading off from the main common area, I saw water fountains and tiled wading pools.

"I guess it makes sense the Arvani officers' club would look like a bathhouse," Boris said. "Are we going to have to go swimming to find the prisoners?"

"No," Ken said, coming back around a corner. "They're all stacked up along the back of this pool."

Five Arvani bodies had been ripped right out of their traveling armor.

"Beached squid," Amira said.

"Yeah." Their long tentacles were coiled like rope in the sand, which had absorbed enough of their spilled fluids to look somewhat jellied.

"That raptor stacked them up nice and pretty," I observed.

"Movement!" Ken shouted.

Something rippled in the water of the common pool. We moved along the wall, Ken and Boris taking point again. The light of the torch dazzled against the walls and rippled reflections in the wavelets past the sand.

"Come out slowly, or we shoot!" Ken shouted on the common channel.

A familiar, mechanically translated "voice" responded. "Who are you?" Ignoring Ken's command, the familiar vision of Commander Zeus rose out of the water in full armor.

"Commander, we're survivors. We came to rescue you."

Zeus paused on the edge of the waterline and swiveled to regard us. The alien instructor took an extra moment to regard Boris's sizzling weapon. "Well, good. We were taken by surprise and with no weapons. My options have been limited. Do you have any plans for what you are going to do next?"

We all looked at each other. "Rescue you, Commander," I said. "And find out if it's just this base under attack, or if everything is. We escaped the Conglomerate attack, along with some others. They have headed for the mining launch facility. We were hoping, at the least, you would know where to find better weapons. Or what we should do next."

"I see." Zeus rotated around quickly and regarded the dead raptor. "This is the spear tip of a Conglomerate attack force. A special swarm, tasked with gaining ground and holding it secretly. They're mopping up anything left alive now. After that will come other cities on the moon in a rapid sequence, directed from this one. Once consolidated, jamming anything in this moon's orbit, they will use the shadow of your moon's orbit to assemble the attack on your world. They likely feel this is less of a waste than a large fleet attack."

"So Earth isn't under attack?" Ken asked. He sounded relieved. Much like me. I was slumping forward, a heavy weight sliding right off my back. I hadn't even realized I was holding that fear so tightly.

"No," Zeus said. "But it will be. If you don't help me. We're going to trigger a self-destruct sequence, maybe take that ship with the base. Together, we can hurt them back. And we're going to send out a distress call that can punch through that jamming."

Fuck. Yeah. I grinned widely. Boris gave me a thumbs-up.

As we moved, Ken paused. "What about the bodies of the

167

other Arvani?" he asked. "Is there anything we should do for them?"

Zeus snorted. "They were lower order Gaskation. Never the best of warriors. Leave them where they lie."

I glanced at Amira.

"A bit cold," she said on the arm's private, encrypted network.

"He's a bastard," I said. "But he's our bastard now."

We followed Zeus to the airlock, buoyed and ready to follow orders. And relieved to have someone who knew what was going on to lead us.

24

We all paused in front of the airlock. I took a deep breath.
Once more back outside, across the surface in the open.

But Zeus stopped us.

"Down," he said. "There are tunnels." Zeus scuttled across
the sand to one of the small wading pools. Spiral stairs on
the other side led down into dimly lit, gray tunnels carved
smoothly out of the lunar rock. How far down had they dug?
The gravity plating had to be under us, and there were grates
and more subsystems handling air and water systems.

Zeus sped up ahead of us. We were adjusting to being
back under the pull of the base's gravity, fine-tuning our suits'
movements.

Armor suddenly slammed into armor when Zeus turned
a corner. Zeus staggered back into sight, suddenly lit up
by a blast of Conglomerate rifle fire as he battled a raptor.
Tentacles writhed and slapped around, and then slowed as
they wrapped around the alien.

"I can't shoot," Ken said. "I'll hit them both."

"Don't," Zeus snapped.

Then, slowly and inexorably, Zeus started pulling the raptor apart.

It looked like the armor strained, bending and buckling slightly as he pushed it to the limit of its abilities. And then, with a popping sound, the raptor's arms came off, the armored surface revealing the flesh inside in an explosion of bodily fluids.

The raptor fell down, writhing.

Zeus kicked it aside with a tentacle, smearing the floor underneath. The useless Conglomerate energy rifle, now bent into a right angle, lay on the floor next to it. Zeus had a long scorch mark running up a tentacle. "That should be it," Zeus said. "Keep following me."

As I stepped over the raptor I paused, looking down at it. The reptilian eyes had clouded over, staring up at the ceiling.

I wondered how intelligent it was. Whether the Conglomeration had designed it to never question what it was doing, or if it believed that flying through the dark of space to come to my world had some greater purpose.

What did it think as it lay there dying?

In the quiet, empty corridors of one of the unused wings, Zeus led us through reinforced locks and into another weapons locker.

A much wider variety of weapons sat on racks here. Sig Sauer P250 handguns. M20 rifles in various configurations, more MP9s, and sturdy Mossburg shotguns.

Since I'd used the submachine gun already, I went for what I knew. Boris lowered his flashlight, staring like a kid in a candy store. "Look at all the RPGs," he whispered. "We have some Sierra-272s."

"GR-50." Ken moved toward a mean, heavy-looking rifle clearly meant for snipers; it was as long as he was tall. "That'll put a dent in some raptor armor."

Zeus clanked to the side where there was a wall of Accordance energy weapons. He picked up a pair of organic matte-black smoothed rifles, similar to the ones we'd trained with, and what looked like battery magazines for them. One of his other tentacles snagged something that looked similar to the Sierra RPG Boris was hugging.

"Okay, Commander," Ken said. "What about the comms now?"

Zeus jerked forward. "Commander," the Arvani mused on the common channel. "I hate that human word."

A tentacle slammed a battery pack into each of the two rifles, while another tentacle slung the longer weapon onto its back.

"I am not a commander, I am not a member of a *human* fighting force. Your ranks are irrelevant to me. I am Cal Riata, a master of the schooling force. And, you idiot of an ape, there is no self-destruct sequence. You will not be calling anyone for help."

Zeus raised the pair of rifles at us.

"What?" Ken said, not moving.

"What building has a self-destruct sequence? Has your home ever had one? Have you ever heard of one of your Navy ships having one?"

All of us, lined up in front of him, being yelled at, shifting from foot to foot: I had a strange sense of déjà vu pass through me in a shiver.

Zeus wasn't done ranting at us. And we all instinctively said nothing. "Or are your military forces genuinely stupid enough to feature an actual sequence that could destroy a fighting asset? That you would believe such a thing existed, that would allow one person to blow up this base, indicates your lesser ability to reason. Now, drop those weapons. Or die standing where you are."

I hadn't even gotten a chance to pick one up yet. Everyone else dropped theirs. I stared at Zeus, my stomach feeling like I was falling as my heart raced.

"You're Conglomerate?" Amira asked. "After all those lectures about how dangerous they are?"

"No. No. I'm Cal Riata," Zeus said, moving forward to flick the weapons on the ground away from us with a tentacle tip. "Proud Cal Riata. One of the finest of the Arvani, sent all the way to this backward system to do the scutwork that's beneath my kind. We Cal Riata lead schools of warships. We rain ruin upon our enemies. But I am here, to be overwhelmed fighting the Conglomeration in rear guard action? No. Not me. And not other Cal Riata who have been forced into positions like this. We are not inclined to be on the losing side."

I had led them into this. I'd decided not to run to the mines. Why had they listened to me? And the others! "Efua," I said on our arm's channel quickly. "Efua. Zeus betrayed us. He's Conglomerate. And he knows about you. Hide, get away. You probably don't have much time."

I wanted to throw up in my helmet. This was bad.

"Shit," Efua said, her voice brittle. "Shit. How long do we have? We're pretty deep inside here."

"You're on the losing side," Zeus continued. "They didn't tell you that, but the Accordance has slowly been watching planet after planet fall to the Conglomeration."

Amira answered Efua. "Not long. There are crickets headed your way. I wish I could tell you more. . . . I'm having trouble sneaking around the network. There's something actively blocking me. I think the Conglomeration has taken over the local networks and has counterintrusion coming online. And some of it is really good, it's blocking me out. I'm sorry."

"So now you kill us?" Ken asked.

"Maybe," Zeus said. "You survived. That shows *some* basic innate intelligence and survival instinct. More than I would have suspected from a bunch of air-breathers. So, quit running around underfoot, messing up plans that took many years to carefully craft, and make something of yourselves. Be rulers. The Conglomeration will need humans to help rule. It could be you."

"And what will you rule?" I asked.

"The Pacific Ocean." Zeus's dinner-plate eyes swiveled to lock onto me. "From the turquoise sandy shallows I will frolic in to the true depths that are my right. The depths my ancestors were chased out of by other Arvani a long, long time ago. What do you want? A state? A small country to rule together? This is the moment where you could have it."

I thought about the acting president, staggering around with his rheumy, alcoholic eyes. "The Conglomeration butchered defenseless recruits," I said.

"Soldiers die in war. It was going to happen, sooner or later," Zeus said. "You were never going to all live through this war. Now, I will take you to answer some questions about the rest of your group, and where they are. You will decide what currents to follow from there. Walk forward now. I'll guide you to where you need to be."

"He could have killed us by now," Boris said. "They want something specific out of us."

"Whatever it is, don't give it to them," Ken said. "Maybe they'll eventually get it out of us, but the longer that takes, the more likely the others get out of the mine."

"Zeus already knows they're in the mines around the launcher," I pointed out. "We told him. There are crickets headed that way. What else could they want? We *gave* them the information they need."

We followed our captor in silence for a moment.

"Plans," Amira said.

"What plans?" Ken asked.

"Zeus said we were upsetting long-laid plans. What plans were there? Plans to take Tranquility and the rest of the moon. They're not sure if we warned anyone or not."

I thought about it. "It could be."

"We might trigger them into attacking earlier," Amira said. "And we haven't actually warned anyone yet. And Efua and her . . . team . . . are going to get attacked."

She'd laid it all out. We'd really fucked this up.

I'd really fucked it up.

"I'm sorry," I told the team. If I could have hung my head visibly, I would have.

"Oh, get over yourself," Amira snapped. "We could have walked away from your plan to come in here and rescue this fucker at any time. It made sense. We rolled with it. You aren't some tragic leader we followed blindly to our deaths. Our eyes were open. We just got screwed by this asshole."

Boris clicked over to the common frequency. "So, you think the Conglomeration is better than the Accordance?" He sounded thoughtful.

"By the depths, no," Zeus said. "The Conglomeration is going to strip your species down to its usable genetic core, and then rebuild you into some tool that serves it best. It's a horrific thing. I have made the best of it."

"So the Conglomeration honors agreements?" Boris asked.

"Boris: What are you asking?" Ken snapped.

"What do we know about these invaders?" Boris asked us on the arm's private channel. "We can be second-class people in the Arvani's Accordance, or we can be lesser peoples within the Conglomeration. Either way, Earth is ruled by another alien race. Maybe we should hear their offer out. Maybe—"

"We know the Conglomeration kills unarmed recruits," I said coldly. "The Accordance, for as much as we hate them, at least follows a rule system. They're conquerors, but they leave us alive and intact once we surrender."

"We don't know what the Conglomeration really is, because all we get is what the Accordance told us," Boris said. "The one thing we do know for sure is that the Accordance is their enemy, and the Accordance rules Earth with a fist."

"The Accordance lifted billions out of war and poverty," Ken hissed. "They—"

Boris interrupted, "You say that because your grand-fathers and great-grandfathers helped that fist, Ken, and you were handed spoils for helping the victors. They built you entire cities and industries in mere months. You didn't grow up watching the Thames run red with blood. . . ."

"Yeah, and why did people in my part of the world need those things so desperately that they would work with aliens, Boris?" Ken shouted. "Because your ancestors were not fuck-ing helping us catch up, after they'd gone so far on our very backs, with *our* resources."

"Divide and conquer," I said softly, breaking in with a soft voice. "And maybe the Conglomeration will do it again, and Londoners will get the keys to the new civil administration. The easiest way to keep a population subjugated is to have them angry with each other. Or . . . maybe everything every creature has ever said about the Conglomeration is right.

I know the struthiform, Shriek, seemed honest enough. I think, maybe the Conglomeration's worse."

A moment's quiet.

"Maybe," Boris agreed. "But I think, to be honest, after the Conglomeration gets what it wants, there won't be a deal. I think we're dead."

"I think you're right," I said.

We trudged on past the ridges of bulkheads and through corridors.

"We're going to have to try and run, or fight him," Ken said. "I refuse to die without fighting."

I'd been thinking. Trying to imagine how I wanted to die. And I knew I agreed with him. I was terrified. But I wanted to do *something*. I didn't want to walk.

But I could see the appeal. Every minute placidly following Zeus meant another minute alive. And the back of my brain wanted life. It saw every minute of continuing life doing this as part of a chain that might mean more life. It was a groove, and I was following it.

How did I want to die? Fighting? Or delaying for every last minute? A placid participant? I wasn't going to try for glory, because it was likely that no one was ever going to know how I died.

But I didn't want to die stupidly. If I was going to try one last thing, let it be clever. Let it be . . .

I put out my right hand and let the tips of my armored fingers tap the bulkhead of another door. "Amira?" I tried not to look up. "Amira, we're passing bulkheads. I know you're cut out, but can you override them?"

She leaned back slightly, then stopped herself. "Shit," she said. "This wing wasn't damaged, so the bulkheads haven't shut automatically. It's too dangerous to open myself up while trying to get into the Accordance network to try to trigger them."

My heart sank. "You can't even try?"

"There's something prowling around it, hunting. I don't know for sure, but I suspect I'll end up a vegetable if I'm not careful."

"Fuck." I clenched a fist. "Is it the ghost? Is that what it is?"

"Maybe. Damn it. There's something familiar about the presence, like it's not Accordance, but I'm feeling like if I had time and the situation was different, I could pick apart the code and find something I've seen before. I don't know, maybe the Accordance stole technology from them and I'm seeing resonances there. But, never mind that . . . ," Amira said thoughtfully. "Maybe I have a way around needing to get into the network."

"We don't have many bulkhead doors left before we're out to the training grounds," I said.

"Shut up. Just a second. I can't get in, but maybe I can trick one locally."

We turned the last bend. The bay doors leading to the training grounds were just a couple hundred feet ahead in the widening corridor.

Amira grunted. "I can shine a laser at the air sensors," she said. "Convince them that everything went to shit. Drop the door. We have to time it just right. We all have to hang back, just a little, but not so much that Captain Calamari here notices."

"Any objections?" I asked.

"Do it," Ken said. We were getting close to another junction where the corridor bisected another. The last bulkhead before the bay doors.

We slowed. Zeus pulled slightly ahead, then stopped and

half turned to look back at us. He suddenly threw the bulk of his armored body back across the junction, his tentacles churning against the metal floor.

The five-inch-thick bulkhead pressure door slammed down into the top of his armor, pinning him to the floor. I had expected him to be on the other side and was caught flat-flooted, not sure whether to run or attack.

"Get his guns!" Ken yelled.

We attacked. Four of Zeus's arms lashed at us, trying to get rifles aimed, while the other four tried to push away from under the door, which had groaned to a halt, lights flashing emergency yellow warning signals. Zeus's skin reacted inside the tank of water, twitching and changing colors like a strobe light. "You fucking apes!"

Zeus shook us around like limp dolls, smacking us against the lip of the pressure door, then against the floor. I tasted salty blood as my head rattled around inside the helmet, my legs fighting to kick a rifle loose as the world snapped dizzyingly around me, then stopped with bone-jarring crunches. "You will die for this. I will flay your skins and use them as *bait*."

When the rifle I'd been kicking at flew across the floor, I continued to hang on, rattling around and trying to hold the tentacle still.

"Got it," Boris said.

"Me too," Ken reported with a clatter.

I let go, smacked into the wall, and staggered back. My armor had been scraped and dented, but still worked.

Zeus dug every single tentacle down into the floor, piercing it and sinking in. Then, slowly, started pulling free of the door.

"Shit."

Amira stepped forward and pointed upward. The pressure door shivered. Smoke drifted from the sides of the walls.

Zeus's tank cracked. The tentacles froze.

The top of the oval tank splintered, and the door lurched down several more inches, cleaving its way in. Blue water slopped out onto the floor, spilling out of the gashes appearing throughout Zeus's armor.

"Do it!" Ken shouted.

Zeus's tentacles started scrabbling again. The back of his armor gurgled, a vomiting sound. Zeus began to frantically pull out of the armor.

The armor gave way in an explosion of fluids, sparks, and screeching. The pressure door slammed into the floor, leaving half a suit and two tentacles in front of us.

We'd been thrown clear of the door by Zeus during the struggle. Boris was the first one to walk forward and lean over the tentacles. "Well, he's going to be limping; there's flesh inside that armor."

"Boris," Amira said in a strangled voice. "Run!"

"What?" He straightened up. I saw his face through the visor. He looked bemused. We'd just won a victory. We'd come back from the brink. Boris wanted a moment.

A blur struck him, moving with inhuman speed from the corridor on the right. It picked him up with ease, as if it were handling a child.

It was an absence of something. Invisible, bending the light around itself and slipping around.

"Ghost!"

They disappeared down the corridor.

"I knew this would come in handy," Boris muttered to the rest of us. "Been saving it for a special occasion. Guys, you'd better run."

"Boris!" I shouted. Amira was picking up one of Zeus's rifles, seeing if she could get it to work. Ken ran forward.

The corridor exploded, knocking Ken back.

"Boris!" Ken screamed, his voice breaking. I couldn't understand whatever he said next. It was in a language I didn't recognize, but a pain in his voice made me shiver. Ken crawled on his hands and knees until I grabbed his ankle.

"We have to run," I said.

Amira grabbed Ken's arm and helped me yank him to his feet, even as he strained to pull away from us.

"We need to get weapons we can use, and get the hell out of here," I said, my voice shaking. "Boris gave us time. Now we need to use it."

25

We had retrieved weapons. The three of us had loaded up everything we could hang off our armor or carry in silence. I had an MP9 hanging from each shoulder, a handgun, and magazines clipped into pinchers up and down my thighs.

Also, after staring at it for a moment, I picked up Boris's cutting torch. Amira paused in front of a shelf, then pulled out what looked like an RPG launcher. But the tube was solid, and ribbed with high-density battery packs and high-energy cabling that crawled in and out of hundreds of ports, giving it a surprisingly cobbled-together look.

I glanced at the labeling on the shelf she'd taken it off. EPC-1 was all it said.

Efua broke the silence as we slowly crawled out over the lunar surface for the ridge that would cover us: the far rim of the Icarus crater. "We're pinned down," she informed us, her voice somewhat flat and calm. "There is a raptor outside, and crickets inside. We're trying to use as little ammunition as we can, but eventually . . . the raptor will come for us."

"We're coming," I said solemnly. "But it's going to take a

181

while to get past the ridge." We were moving from shadow to shadow again, easing our way over the pockmarked surface out of the line of sight of the Conglomerate ship.

"And how long do you think 'a while' might be?" Efua asked.

"It took five hours to cross last time," Amira said. "Plus time to get from the ridge to the mines."

"Five hours," Efua repeated. "Okay. Okay, six hours. We will see you then."

She didn't sound sure of that. She was talking herself into it.

"The ghost isn't dead," Amira whispered. "It's still on the Accordance networks, trying to find me. I have to stay locked down."

"It could be a different ghost," Ken said, speaking for the first time in over an hour.

"It *could* be," Amira agreed. She didn't sound sure.

"Trolls," I said from my spot in the dark. The giant creatures had come around the side of the base, roving back and forth in a crude search pattern.

"They're going to slaughter everyone in Tranquility," Ken said, two hours later. We crouched in separate craters, waiting for the trolls to turn their backs so we could move. "And then they'll come for Earth."

"I know." I was in the clear. I scrabbled over broken rock to leap out from the shadows in the dark. I landed on the tip of a boulder, then swung behind it just before a troll turned and looked my way.

No dust, I pleaded. It had been a long, risky move.

"It didn't see you," Amira said.

I let out a breath.

"Clear to spot for me," she said a moment later.

I peeked around the boulder and got eyes on both massive aliens.

"What are we going to do?" Ken asked.

"Stay alive," I said. "Try to get word out. Try to walk out from under this jamming and get Amira to send a message. And you're good, Amira. Go."

I saw Amira kangaroo out from boulder to boulder in almost a straight line. The impacts looked brutal, but it kept her from arcing up high over the surface.

Smart. I'd have to try that.

"It's going to take too long to walk out from under this," Ken said. "They will move away and attack Tranquility before we have a chance to get within range of something that can hear our suits. We need to take direct action."

"You're welcome to pop up and wave at the trolls anytime you want," I told him. "I don't want to be toe-paste."

"There is more than just surviving," Ken snapped. "The stakes are much higher."

"Stay alive first," Amira cautioned. "The longer we do, the more options we can scare up."

"I just . . . ," Ken started.

"I know," Amira said. "Save that. Just hold on to it for later."

I leaned back against the boulder and looked up over the ridge that we'd been slowly, too slowly, moving closer to.

Something twinkled up into the dark sky between a notch in the rock, then disappeared, blocked from my sight as it was flung into orbit.

"Efua, Devlin here," I said. "Is the mass driver still launching payloads?"

"Devlin, I hear you, just one moment." Efua grunted. The sound of something like a slap came through, and tortured metal. Efua panted. "Yes. It just launched. I think the Conglomeration is leaving it alone, so that no one from Tranquility realizes anything is wrong over here."

No gunshots. Her team had to be attacking crickets by their armored hands to save ammunition.

Dangerous. But they were trapped and running low.

Buying time, I thought. All we were doing was buying time. And the end was the same no matter what. We were not going to live through this. Even if we got word out, or hid and survived, eventually our air would run out.

We needed to go about this in a different direction. We needed to stop running and start *thinking*.

I looked back up at the notch where the twinkle of the launch came through.

"I think Ken's right," I said, before I'd even realized it.

"Shit. You too?" Amira sighed. "What are you thinking now? We storm the base?"

"No. We're fucked," I told her. "We're outnumbered. We'd get cut down the moment we popped our heads up. But maybe we can still hurt them. Hurt them enough to get a signal out. When Zeus flew us in, he said the mass driver could change where it delivered packages."

"It's giant artillery," Amira said. "Right in front of us. You're right. But there is a raptor and a shitload of crickets crawling around."

"I didn't say it would be easy. Or guaranteed. But can you access the systems?"

"That's not the biggest problem," Amira said.

What had I missed? "What's the problem?"

"The moment I get into the Accordance systems on that thing, the ghost will know. It's sniffing everything around here. I see why the Accordance uses entangled quantum systems for our team comms, and tries to use regular frequencies as little as possible. Trolls aren't looking, you're a go."

"Moving." I took a deep breath and shot across the surface and up the ridge. I smacked into rocks, some of them tumbling down the base-facing side. "Shit."

On the other side I rabbited again.

"They're focused elsewhere, still good. Still good. Ken: Go!"

I found a bolt-hole on the other side of the slope and watched the horizon.

"Can you trick it?" I asked.

"Go," Ken said.

Amira responded with a grunt. She was moving now. I looked left just in time to see her somersault over the ridge and arc slowly down into the crater. She hit in a plume of dust.

"Get clear of that," Ken said.

She hopped from rock to rock, away from dirt, trying to avoid leaving tracks from the large divot she'd made. "What do you mean, 'trick it'?"

"They're going to know we're attacking and retaking the mass driver and the mines supplying it," I said. "So they're not going to be *that* surprised if you show up on the network. I don't know a ton about systems and networks, but can you trick them into thinking you're trying to break out a signal?"

Amira bounced around some more, then came to a stop. "Maybe," she said thoughtfully.

"As long as they don't realize we're fucking with the mass driver," I said. "We hit their ship, the jamming goes down, we warn everyone."

"And then all hell breaks loose."

"Exactly," I said. "And a lot of lives might be saved."

"We are clear," Ken said, arcing overhead in a long jump

away from the rim. "They are circling back the other way. And I think Devlin has the plan."

"My last one wasn't so hot," I said.

Ken hit dirt. "I want to see that seething mass of Conglomerate shit fall out of the sky and burn. I can't think of any other way to make that happen, and it's a better plan than any I've come up with. Amira, are you willing?"

"You can't do this without me," she said.

"It matters how we choose to die," Ken said.

"Don't lecture me about how to die, Ken. I've seen people throw themselves at a cause and bleed out in the street. I've held arms while basement surgeons try to save a fighter for a cause. When the moment comes, all you have is pain and fear. No one's marching off into it full of fervor and excitement. They beg for their mothers. They beg for relief."

"They scream," Ken agreed softly. "Then they choke, because the air is sucked out of the building. You try to give them air, but some of them wave you away. And then their heads pop, hit by concentrated energy. Hundreds of them. No fervor, Amira. Just survival."

"I'm sorry," she said. "I forgot you were in there when it happened."

"And so was Boris," Ken said. "I want to give them back a taste of what they did. Will you help?"

"Well, we're going to head over there to help Efua out anyway," Amira said. "We might as well try this."

"Good." I stood up and loped along behind them. "Efua, we're coming!"

"I heard your plan," she said. "But you need to hurry."

We picked up the pace as best we could.

26

Crickets swarmed around the pilings, a mechanized cloud of snapping pincers and needle-sharp maws. The launcher itself dwarfed us all. It sat inside a low-lying crater, the breech down at the center and the tip propped up by the ridge a mile away. Accordance engineers had then covered the entire crater in superstructural, organic latticework that created a perfect bowl for the barrel to rest in.

The mile-long barrel could be moved, just as Zeus had said. The lattice below it had gears and pistons the size of buildings under the pilings. A typical Accordance structure: fragile looking, giant, and carved quickly out of a landscape.

"Where are the tunnels to the mines?" Ken asked. "Efua? Can you tell us?"

"She's been quiet for the last forty minutes," Amira said.

"Efua!" Ken repeated.

"She'll answer us if she can," I said.

"Let's try the base of the launcher," Amira said. "There's probably another way in. They'd want to be able to drive things in, but we'll have to walk all the way around the rim of the crater to find it. They have to have something near all that equipment that needs maintaining, though."

"Also, that's where the crickets are swarming from," I agreed. The moving cloud hadn't spotted us peeking down from the ridge at them yet. A small part of me suggested that it would be a good idea to turn and run before they did, that I could still live through this by running.

But where?

"We have to be quick; they could just cluster and over-whelm us." Amira sounded annoyed by the idea, like it was a tactic beneath her.

"Keep them away from your helmet," Ken said. "Don't waste too much of your ammunition. And watch for the raptor. I haven't spotted it yet, have any of you?"

A child-sized cricket scuttled up from under the latticework and leapt into the air. Amira fired once with a handgun, hitting it in the center and scattering pieces, which rained slowly down around us.

The boiling mass at the center of the crater stopped swirling around the mass driver's infrastructure and swirled in our direction.

"Let's go!" I shouted, leaping over the ridge and onto the lattice toward the swarm. "Amira, keep behind us."

"Oh, bullshit," she snapped, angry. I looked up as she leapt over me toward the oncoming rush.

"You're the only one that can program the damn thing!" I shouted.

"Then keep up." Amira jumped again, high and visible to the cricket swarm. They adjusted en masse, shifting to antici-pate where she would land.

"Amira!"

At the apex of her jump she swapped from handgun to the

EPC-1 device with all the energy blisters she'd slung on her back. And didn't fire.

It had been a ridiculously tall jump, with not much forward progress. Crickets boiled underneath her, climbing over each other's metallic jointed bodies with artificial eagerness to look upward at her. Jaws snapped, legs readied to stab at her.

Ken changed course, headed toward the growing mountain of crickets. "Get back," Amira snapped as she plummeted down at them.

She triggered the device she held casually at her hip. The energy blisters glowed, the cabling lit up, sparked, and a ring of energy spat from the tip. Everything in my suit dimmed slightly at the same time, and my movements stuttered.

Crickets of various sizes and shapes fizzled and spat, then fell still. Amira plunged into their bodies and slid down a hill of twitching legs. "They're not the only ones who can use electromagnetic pulses," she said triumphantly. "Electronic Pulse Cannon, model 1, for the win. Come on!"

We changed course, zigging and zagging our way down the slope so that crickets could gather and clump for Amira. After two more bursts, and two more piles of twitching crickets, we hit the base.

"So many," I muttered.

"At least we haven't encountered any drivers," Amira said. Just the test ones in training could scatter us.

"Don't jinx us like that." I didn't even want to think of the things jamming their tails into my spine to take me over.

"There's an airlock, and a ramp," Ken said, veering off.

"Right behind you," Amira said.

I came up behind them, making sure something didn't get us while we entered. Amira hopped around, looking for manual overrides.

Three cat-sized crickets, one of them dragging broken legs behind it, leapt over the ramp's edge at us. I shot them down with a few silent, quick bursts of my MP9, then crushed the remains with my heel.

"Okay," Amira said. "We're in."

We piled into the airlock and Amira shut it behind us. Moments later things clattered against it, trying to break through and get to us.

We stood in the space between the two doors for a moment, catching our breath.

Then Amira grabbed a lever and pumped it several times to charge the inner door. "You ready for this?" she asked.

I raised my MP9. "Yes."

I was lying. Anything on the other side knew something was about to come through.

Ken stepped up next to me. "Ready," he said.

Amira pushed the lever back into the wall and the door clunked, then jerked open. A white-hot bolt of lightning blew my vision out as it snapped through the open space and hit Ken. He opened fire even as he flew back, knocked into the outer door.

I stepped forward, firing wildly. Amira's weapon fired, my steps stuttered, and fuzzy static filled my ears. "Got the energy rifle," she said.

The snap of electricity stopped, my helmet visor faded, and my sight returned just in time for me to see a raptor in midleap, tossing its now-ruined weapon to the side.

"Raptor!" Ken shouted, a moment too late.

"Oh—" It struck me, knocking me right back into the airlock. "Shit!"

The thwack of bullets filled the airlock: Amira, on the raptor's back, firing point-blank at its long neck with her handgun. It let go of me and slammed up against the airlock, trying to shake her loose.

Ken staggered to his feet as I fumbled with the welder. I'd seen Boris use it, but it was an alien tool designed for alien hands. For several agonizing seconds, I couldn't figure out how to turn it on as we struggled in the airlock.

Then it lit up, the points converging on the pure point of light, and I swung it up into the tangle of Amira, Ken, and the raptor. I aimed for its chest, but Ken, wrestling with one of its hands, swept past me. The welder cut through his calf and he screamed.

"Shit." I apologized as I slammed the torch into the raptor's chest, not willing to risk also hitting Amira, who struggled on its shoulders, if I aimed for the neck.

Molten armor splashed back against me and covered my shielded wrists. I shoved forward, and the raptor staggered back. "Get away," I warned Amira as I leaned in, feeling the welder bite through armor, then pop through.

Amira rolled away, and I pinned the alien to the wall and buried the weapon deeper with another shove. It stopped trying to claw at me. It slumped forward, pinned as the welder passed through the back of its armor and melted into the wall.

"I think you got it," Amira said. "You can turn it off."

I pulled my thumb off the button and the sizzling faded. I let go, leaving both the alien and the welder hanging from the wall, and turned around. "Ken!"

He stood on one leg, with an arm over Amira's shoulder. "I'm okay," he said, through audibly gritted teeth. I could see sweat dripping from his face through his helmet.

"Shit, man, I'm so fucking sorry."

"You killed it." He grimaced. "That is what matters. And the cut is not so bad. The suit is giving me painkillers and

191

packing the wound with sealant. I can compensate. You can let me go. We must get control of the mass driver."

He pulled away from Amira and wobbled on his own.

"I just need somewhere to patch in locally," Amira said. She sounded tired. They were all running on fumes. Maybe even making mistakes at this point. Small ones, but how straight could you think when you hadn't slept since the attack?

But we couldn't slow anything down now.

"There will be more crickets in here," Ken said. "Go with Amira so she can focus on the things she needs to do. I'll search for Efua and the others."

"Be careful." I wanted to grab his forearm, but he nodded and limped down the corridor. I turned and grabbed the welder with both hands and yanked it. The raptor toppled to the floor.

"This way," Amira said, stepping over it.

"How do you know?"

She pointed to the floor. "Directions in ultraviolet, lines that lead to different points. I can read a little Arvani."

We leapfrogged sloppily and quickly down the corridor, grateful for no surprises but still jumpy in the low red lighting.

Several turns later and a floor below, Amira triggered a set of doors. "Here we go."

Floor-to-ceiling displays cascaded information, including outside views of the launcher. "I thought there'd be *something* in here," I said.

"Shit's automated," Amira said. "This room's for trouble-shooting and maintenance. Watch the doors."

I set up next to them, glancing back at her as she walked to one of the displays and put her palm out. Blue light danced across her arm. "The clock just started," she said. "The ghost knows we are here."

Her fingers began to twitch as she manipulated glyphs in the air.

"Does it know what you're doing?"

"Shhhh. It thinks we're trying to signal out. The jamming just kicked way up."

She went back to work. I kept quiet. But there was a new noise. I amplified it. A sound like metal hail against the outer door.

Crickets trying to get in.

I had to assume she'd locked them out. How many had piled up out there, redirected by the ghost to come knocking?

I swallowed. What else might come join them at the door as I waited.

"I found Efua and the others," Ken said. I could hear in his voice what he was seeing, by the way it cracked slightly and in the soft tone.

"I'm sorry, man." I shook my head. "I'm sorry."

"Amira?" Ken asked sadly.

A long pause. "They're dead?" Amira asked.

"Yes."

She sounded as shattered as Ken did. "I can't do it."

"What do you mean?" Ken and I asked her as one.

"The mountain in the center of that crater the base is in. It's in the way. I can't take out the ship, or them, or the base. I guess I could shoot at the top of the ridge and hope something gets through, but I doubt it. And it'll warn them. They'll have time to move. And I can't aim the launcher higher, like artillery. And that wouldn't work anyway; the moon's gravity is too weak. No matter where you point that fucker, the payload's going to orbit. I'm so sorry, guys. We can't turn it and shoot."

I wanted to slide down, my legs felt so suddenly weak. Out on the other side of the door, the sound of the metallic hail slowly grew louder and more insistent.

27

I looked at the screen that Amira waved into existence. It showed the mass of rock in our way. Not something any of us had thought about: topography. And I'd assumed she could have fired *over* anything. But the gravity was too weak on the moon. Things fired at great speed took a while to curve downward.

Ken made a strangled, frustrated sound. I couldn't blame him.

"We need to get out of here," Amira said.

"No." I held up a hand. "No. We need to brainstorm. We need to slow down. All three of us. There has to be an answer here."

"Damn it," Amira snapped. "Let go of it. We're not going to be heroes. We're not going to save the day. Even if this had worked, we were probably going to die like Efua, trapped in a corridor somewhere. Let's find a place to buy more time, Devlin."

"Take a breath," I said. "You're tired, we've fought these things since we broke into the base. We're still alive, but we're running on adrenaline and will. Let's not make a mistake now, when we've come so far. Come on, let's just stop. We have a launcher—"

"Fire a series of them," Ken suggested. "First one blows up the hilltop. The next one comes through."

"I thought about that," Amira said wearily. "First explosion alerts them. They move."

"Not necessarily," Ken replied.

"No, but I also don't know for sure if the hilltop will break away. It's soft. It might just create a hell of a dust cloud and that's it. I can't model what's going to happen without more time and computing. We're not going to get that. So that's two unknowns."

Small dents were being hammered into the door. A single feeler rammed its way through the gap between the doors, trying to pry them open. I broke it off and stomped on it.

"We have a device that can launch anything we want into orbit," I said. "What else can we do? Launch ourselves? Can you slow it down so we're not instant toothpaste?"

"Wait," Amira said. "Wait a second."

I had a vision of us in armor, in orbit, beaming a weak SOS to anyone who could hear us. "Or maybe we could put an emergency signal on repeat on a suit and put that into orbit," Ken said. "We don't have to load ourselves. We . . . have extra armor here."

"No. Shut up." Amira had her hands up behind her neck. "Orbit. It's about orbit." She was thinking. But we were all so tired.

"What?" A series of loud pops against the doors made me jump. Something fizzled outside. What the hell were the crickets doing out there?

"Orbit." Amira's fingers danced again. She stood in front

of the lights and glyphs like a conductor. Lines flowered out from a central point in the air. "Fucking orbit!"

"This is good, right?" Ken asked. "You have an idea?"

"I hate to say it, but Devlin's right. I was too tired to see it. We're still going to shell the fuck out of that Conglomerate ship." Amira sounded excited.

"How?"

"We're not going to fire right at them, we're going to come at them from behind," Amira said. "The capsules will fire into orbit, all around the moon, and then hit from the other direction. Each capsule contains a ton of ore, and it's going to be moving fast. Each shot will be a slightly different angle, so when it comes back around, it's going to saturate the area. And all at the same fucking time, too."

"Will the ship have time to get away?" I asked. "If the shots come in from orbit."

"Not if I come in low, just above the surface. The moon is very round, it's smaller. I can use topography maps, the first rounds can come in right over the hills. The ship will have seconds to react at the speeds I'm planning."

"I like this," Ken said. "How long will it take to do this?"

"Not long. First capsule just got fired, and it looks good. Just keep those crickets out of the room and I'll start. But we'll need to stay in here until the capsules hit," Amira said.

"Why?"

"The capsules can maneuver. Small adjustments, but if the Conglomeration figure out what we did, they could alter the commands, shift where the rounds hit to somewhere else nearby. If we hold the room, there's a better chance."

I looked at the door. Another small leg had wiggled through and was waving about. I crushed it. "It's going to be dicey."

"All we have to do is last until the capsules come back around. Two hours."

"Two hours." I shook my head. Stay alive for two hours.

More dents appeared in the door.

Maybe.

"Oh . . . ," Amira breathed. "That's not good."

"What?"

She waved one of the images through the air toward me. "Trolls."

Two of them softly trudged through the dirt on the other side of the ridge, a mile away and closing. Crickets loped along with them, some riding on the large, irregular feet.

Farther back, three raptors arced through the lunar night in a triangular formation.

"Reinforcements," I told Ken. "The two trolls. Three raptors. More crickets."

"And the ghost is out there somewhere," Amira said. "I can feel it. Probing. Trying to figure out what I'm up to."

I looked around the room. "When I leave the room, you hide in the floor panels. Crickets can't see you, or they'll report back there's still someone in here. They have to think it's just me and Ken that'll be running around outside."

"It's too dangerous out there," Amira said. "The ghost—"

"Don't use that electromagnetic pulse cannon unless you have to, if you're holding the room. We want to get as much time keeping them guessing as we can," I continued.

"I won't stay in here." Amira raised her hands.

"You have to," I pleaded. "You're systems. You have to make it through this. You have to make sure these fuckers get the hammer dropped on them."

"Fuck!" Amira shouted.

She was right. Running would feel better than hiding and

waiting. It was not her style to hole up in the shadows. But she needed this room. "I'm so sorry. We need to hold the room. We need to pull them away."

"Okay," she said. "Okay. I can power down the suit, hide under the cable runs. I should be able to sneak into the system here and there, keep monitoring things. I'll keep the EPC, if I have to, last ditch, hold the room. Damn it, you two give them a hell of a chase, okay? And we meet up afterward."

"You two are stuck with me for a long while yet." I helped her rip the flooring up. She crawled in, digging down between thick conduit and cables, then I handed her the EPC.

I pushed the floor back down, making sure the panels fit right in and didn't look disturbed.

Crossing my fingers mentally, I approached the doors.

"Be careful," Amira said. "Tell me when to open them."

"Yeah. Careful," I said. I took a deep breath. "Open."

The doors jerked open and crickets poured over each other to get inside at me. I opened fire and leapt through into the boiling mass, yanking clutching limbs free and swearing.

28

I slid around a corner, a wave of crickets nipping at my heels.

"Duck," Ken growled. He stepped around the next corner and raised an MP9 in each hand. I slid, and he opened fire. The chattering sounded distant through my helmet, but I could feel cricket bits and pieces pinging against my armor.

Ken dropped the submachine guns to swap to a handgun as he jumped over me and started smashing remaining crickets against the wall.

They swirled around, keeping away from him, then changed direction and scuttled away in full retreat.

I stood up as Ken limped back my way.

"Now to get outside," he said to me. "And lead them all away. Amira, are you still hidden?"

"Yeah." It was a curt, chopped off "yeah." "Want me to take a look at how close your guests are?"

"Take no risks," Ken said.

Ken and I got into the airlock. We stood on either side of the scorched body of the raptor. Three more of those things

199

were coming for the two of us, I thought. And one almost killed the three of us. "What about your leg?" I asked. "I cut through, didn't I?"

"There was sealant both for my leg, and to secure integrity," Ken said. "It should be fine."

"Should be?"

"Yes." Ken pumped the manual lever, and the door leading back to the corridor shuddered shut.

"Because now's the time for you to turn back," I said.

"Why would I turn back?" Ken asked, incredulous.

"So you don't die out there on the lunar surface when that outer door opens."

Ken stepped forward with a thud and pumped the outward manual lever. "We're hoping they haven't noticed there were three of us, and Amira makes sure to destroy their ship, and many of them. As for you and me . . ." The outer door slid open with a rush of air.

We leapt out, weapons up. But nothing shot back at us. No giant feet stomped us out of existence.

"They're still coming," I said, relieved.

Ken bounded up the latticework alongside the giant barrel. "Come on," he urged.

We hopped and bounced our way up, huffing and puffing until we reached the rim and stopped to look back.

"How's the leg?" I asked.

"The seal holds," Ken replied. We stood on the rock, watching the other side. Waiting.

"Shit, this is intolerable," I said. "My hands are shaking. Just standing here. Jumpy."

"My father fought in the Pacification," Ken said. "He said a lot of war is just standing, waiting for the sudden action that might mean your death."

I guessed Ken's father hadn't been fighting the Accordance. But I didn't say anything, just kept looking at the ridge.

"There." The two trolls crested the other side and paused.

Ken reached back, then flung a grenade that had been stuck to his lower back. It arced accurately over the length of the barrel, across the crater to the other side, and skittered across near the trolls' feet.

Their large heads swiveled our way as the grenade exploded, charring the lattice but not them. One of the wormhole cannons snapped up. Ken and I both leapt away. The rock where we'd stood shivered as it was stripped clean of dirt, then a large chunk ripped free and flew away.

"That got their attention." I hopped around boulders. "Should we split up?"

"No. But be silent. This is now a marathon." Ken sailed away with a giant leap.

I followed.

We fell into a rhythm, an awkward-looking set of jumps alternating leg to leg, assisted by the armor. Occasionally Ken would accidentally key the channel, and I'd hear him grunt in pain as he landed on his left leg and jumped.

I didn't say anything.

We ate up several miles this way, sometimes pausing when one or the other fumbled and wiped out in the dirt. The adaptive camouflage didn't do too much good with this much movement, but after forty minutes on the run we were gray, dirty messes that had to be hard to spot from a distance.

Problem was, the trolls weren't that far in the distance. They were gaining. Every minute they loomed even closer, and the raptors were just behind them.

"When do we make our stand?" I asked, scanning for good

terrain. Some rabbiting, turning around, maybe we could get our hands on one of the raptors.

Maybe.

"I see a lot of jagged hills to the north," Ken said. "Lets—" A blur struck him right at the apex of his jump. He tumbled end over end with it, grappling as they rolled.

I swerved toward them, trying not to look behind us. The trolls would get within wormhole cannon range in twenty seconds easy. I keyed the welder on, lighting up the gray lunar surface with its pure light, tossing shadows everywhere.

Every ounce of me strained as I leapt from a boulder, arrowing right at Ken. I aimed the tip of energy right at the blur, despite not being able to even understand what I was seeing.

"What's happening?" Amira asked. "Is it the ghost?"

At the last second the slippery nothingness twitched. I struck it hard enough to knock Ken loose and started trying to stab it with the welder. It had penetrated raptor armor; maybe it would cut through this. "Run, Ken!" I could feel the ground underneath me shake.

"Guys?"

The nothingness had my wrists. I struggled to pivot the welder, but my wrists were pushed back, and then farther back, until something tore and popped and I couldn't hold the welder anymore.

The welder dropped to the ground and spat dust until something turned it off.

I lay pinned to the ground, looking right through whatever held me there, to the darkness far above. I waited for the killing shot, or blow, but nothing happened. The blur picked me up, and then, slowly, began to walk.

The camouflage on the ghost worked similarly to the

Accordance's: It was bending light around itself to replicate whatever was on the other side. This close, I could see the effect shifting in real time. Accordance armor required you to stay still, but this armor adjusted in time to keep the effect going. And even at six inches away, all I could tell was that the ghost was bipedal.

Whatever was underneath, I still couldn't see.

"Ken?" Amira asked.

"I'm sorry," Ken said. "He saved me from the ghost. But now . . ."

"I'm not dead yet," I said, and then, utterly perplexed, I added, "It's carrying me. Tell my parents—"

"I'm going to come for you!" Ken interrupted.

"No!" I twisted around to look. "The trolls are following me and the ghost, but the raptors are still out looking for you. Wherever you're hidden, just stay put. We're keeping them out of Amira's way still, there's nothing you can do for me."

"But I can," Amira said. "You're far enough downrange of the launcher that I might be able to fire on you. I could get the capsules to start maneuvering right out of the barrel to arc down at you and hit the trolls."

"No," I said firmly. "That will warn them that we have control of the launcher. No, let it take me."

"Damn it," Amira snapped. "Listen, give me access to your suit. Just think permission my way, I want in."

"What will that accomplish?"

"Just do it. I've been thinking about the ghost. The Conglomeration, they're thinking creatures. They use machines. And that has to mean similarities. They have assembly language, or ones and zeroes, or something. Input-output ports."

"Can you explain that in plain English?" Ken asked.

"There are maybe even similarities in technology," Amira

continued, and then paused. "Ken, I'm going to use his suit to probe the area around him using our encrypted connection. Thankfully it's impossible for them to tell we're talking over quantum networks."

"Okay, Amira," I said. And willed the permission over my neural connection.

"What do you think you can do?" Ken asked.

Hopefully she would learn something about our enemy, I thought. I looked over at the massive, rock-armored feet of the trolls.

And maybe she could figure out why they were taking me alive.

29

The trolls continued their honor guard position all the way back to the ruins of the base. We stopped under the trailing arms of the jellylike Conglomerate starship. Two raptors ran out of a nearby airlock, danced around the trolls, and tried to grab me. The ghost responded, invisible limbs shoving one of them rudely back.

"You stopped moving," Amira said. "Are you okay?"

"There are two raptors here." They aimed their energy rifles at me. "They seem to be arguing with the ghost."

"About what?"

"I don't know. I don't speak invisible alien," I snapped. "But I think maybe they want me dead."

A massive hand swung from the sky and slapped a raptor. It flew across the dirt and bounced several times, and the second troll stepped forward and crouched aggressively in front of the other raptor.

It slung its rifle and stepped back.

The other raptor stood up and visibly shook itself, then slunk off.

"I've been working hard on updating some heads-up display software to patch in and show you something," Amira said. "You're going to need it. You're in the strike zone and you have five minutes before the barrage starts."

"I'm not getting away," I said. I'd been fighting the ghost all the way here. In addition to broken wrists, I now had contusions all over my body. A slight concussion from rattling my head around left me slightly out of it. The ghost was stronger and faster.

My visor flickered and rebooted. The information about my suit and charge levels faded. It came back on, and the lunar surface around me changed. It was overlit by large pools of red light.

"Red is impact, timers are above them. The arcs are the trajectories."

A four-minute timer hung above the red bull's-eye I stood in. I looked above me. Three minutes until the Conglomerate ship got hit. Lines of silvery thread led away from the center of the impact pools off into the dark sky.

Nine different silver lines led to the alien ship. Another ghostly one appeared as I watched. Each came in from a different angle or vector.

"Now, for getting you away from the ghost, I need you to hug it and get the charge port in your heels firmly against its surface. I'm going to discharge your power into it, and when I do that, it will temporarily overwhelm it. Or startle it. I hope. It's the best I can do."

She sounded so apologetic, I felt duty-bound to respond with energy. But I was tired, and hurting, even despite the painkillers I'd had the suit pump into me. "Thank you, Amira." I looked up. Two minutes.

"If that happens, you run. Stay out of the red zones. Debris is still an issue. You'll have to work hard, the suit will be mostly dead or dying after the discharge of energy."

"Okay."

One of the long tentacles unfurled itself from the starship and reached down for the ground. I watched it descend all the way down to meet us. The flat tip hit the ground in front us, kicking up lunar dust. I gently shifted my feet down, angling them to touch the ghost's invisible surface.

"Tell me when you're ready," Amira said.

Sixty seconds.

The ghost and trolls waited for the dust to settle, then stepped forward onto the flat tip of the tentacle. I pressed my boots firmly against the ghost.

Forty seconds.

The tentacle contracted, transparent musculature showing veins the size of bridge cables pumping fluid underneath its skin, and we slowly rose.

I watched the lunar surface drop away.

Thirty seconds.

"Now," I told Amira.

My boots exploded with arcs of electricity. The ghost danced and writhed in pure blue light, and its viselike grip on me broke.

I shoved off and out from the platform tip of the tentacle and into free fall, streaming electricity as I fell.

When I hit the ground on my back I lay there, the air knocked out of my chest, gasping.

Fifteen seconds. "Did it work?" Amira asked.

"Yes," I hissed. One of the trolls let go of the tentacle and stepped out over the side to fall down after me. I got up. The armor wasn't too heavy, but there was no assistance. It was just me and my own muscle.

The troll struck the ground in front of me.

I turned and ran back the other way in a halfhearted loping bounce. I just needed to get out from under the ship, even if it meant heading farther into the strike zones. The pool I stood in had a countdown of a minute.

Seven seconds. A troll leapt over me and landed in front of me. We faced off.

Five.

It stopped looking at me and glanced up.

Three, two.

One. Something flashed along the silver line so quickly I barely saw it and struck the side of the Conglomerate ship. The entire jellylike structure shivered as the capsule ripped out the other side. Debris hung in the air over us, yanked out of the ship's insides. "It's a hit!" I shouted, and regretted it. Pain spiked through my ribs from the effort.

A figure leapt out away from the tentacle. It was no longer invisible; I could see limbs. Two legs, two arms, a head. The flat gray armor looked mundane now.

The second impact and third hit the Conglomerate ship. It began to move, wobbling and struggling to get away.

"Devlin, run!"

I turned and bounced away, looking at the red pools. Twenty seconds. I veered in a circle, leading the troll around and into it. The now visible ghost followed. I'd burned out its camouflage and gotten away, but it was mobile again. And coming for me. Shit.

Ten.

Amira shouted excitedly. "Kinetic energy is an *angry* bitch!"

The ship was no longer directly overhead and debris was hitting the ground everywhere, pieces of the ship falling away. A whole tentacle detached and draped itself over the base.

Crickets boiled out from the ship and the base, leaping and running for safety.

"Devlin, Ken? Are you okay?"

I doubled back, away from the next target. The troll followed. I stopped at the edge, turned back to it, and raised my hands. The ghost stepped forward, out from under the troll's legs.

The lunar surface exploded as the impact I was waiting for happened. I flew through the air, cartwheeling hard enough to black out, then jar back to life as I struck the surface. I bounced several times.

There was no troll anymore, just a black stain where it had stood. Impacts were hitting constantly, the ground shaking every few seconds as payloads Amira had sent up in various orbits were all now converging to hit at almost the same time, even though they'd been launched at different intervals.

The ghost had been flung with me. It lay still, arms and legs spread at unnatural angles. I crawled over, glancing around at the impact points on Amira's heads-up display to see if it was safe as I worked my way toward safety. Sixty seconds before this area would get hit by another of Amira's capsules.

I looked at the ghost as I passed by, and froze.

His face was covered in blood.

But it was a he.

It was a person.

There was a dead *human being* in Conglomerate armor lying on the ground. The ghost was human.

Was this a trick? What did it mean? Had Conglomerate forces been to Earth? When? Or was it some kind of parallel evolution?

Or was this Conglomerate species molded to look human so it could invade or rule Earth?

I didn't know. I grabbed the body and pulled it along with me, grateful for the lower gravity.

Thirty seconds.

I stumbled and fell as I ran out of the area as best I could and—

Wham!

—another impact threw me clear as I clutched the ghost's body. Rocks and dirt rattled against my armor.

I scrabbled along farther, getting clear of the impact zones. I was on my ass, pulling the ghost after me. I watched the Conglomerate ship fall slowly into the base, vomiting gas and fire as it burned and I scooted slowly away.

My heads-up display flickered and died.

No air scrubbing now. I would just breathe the air left inside until I passed out. I wasn't sure how long that would be, but I was sure it wasn't long enough for me to make it back to the launcher.

I sat on top of the ghost, hoping it was truly dead, and watched the destruction unfold in front of me.

30

"Are you okay?" Ken had to push his helmet's visor against mine for sound to travel between us. A quick and crude way for us to communicate. Sound waves hitting his visor, then mine, then passing back to me. He sounded distant and tinny. "Devlin, say something."

I coughed.

"Amira, he's okay. He has some air still."

But not for much longer, I thought.

"Hold on, Amira gave me an air canister when she sent me to look for you," Ken said. He left and walked around to my side. A loud hiss startled me, and then my head cleared. Fresh air. My apathy at seeing Ken, at still being alive, was swept away.

But with that came the awareness of all the pain I was in. And I couldn't request a new round of painkillers.

Ken came back around and touched helmets again. "I think we can make it to the launcher now. Who is that with you? Is he alive?"

"It's the ghost," I said. "Help me pick it up. My wrists are broken."

"But . . ." Ken pulled away to look closer. He turned back to me, talking, but I couldn't hear him without our helmets touching.

He grabbed my helmet and bumped his visor into mine again. "It's a person."

"I know." I pulled away and tried to reach for the ghost on my elbows and knees. Ken shook his head and picked it up. He slung it over his shoulder and leapt ahead of me.

Of course, his armor was still functional. I struggled to my feet, hard to do without using my hands, and bounded after him as best I could on complaining muscles.

We made better time to the launcher than we had when hiding from the Conglomeration, even though I was slowing Ken down. Nothing swarmed us as we bounced over craters and scrambled up the hills.

Amira waited by the slopes of the launcher's crater. She leapt into our midst and tapped me, then pointed up.

Silver Accordance ships, lean and festooned with shards and spikes that indicated heavy energy weaponry descended from overhead.

The cavalry, it seemed, had arrived.

Armored struthiforms jumped out of opening bay doors and down to the ground. They swarmed over us, knocking us down to the dirt and trussing us with electrified cables that snapped and spat as they touched our armor.

I screamed as my wrists were wrenched tight.

They didn't know what was going on, I told myself. All they know is that the base is destroyed.

The cables were hooked to something that reeled us right up off the ground into the nearest hovering ship. Within seconds we were surrounded by more aggressive struthiforms, who stripped our armor off.

"Get away from the armor," they shouted.

"We are the good guys," Ken protested, and got struck in the face. He fell down, bleeding.

Amira twitched, but I shook my head. "Don't. Don't do anything. Just stay still."

"Be quiet!"

"If I get put in a cell after saving *all your asses* I'm going to be really fucking pissed off," Amira shouted.

One of the struthiforms raised an energy rifle, and Amira turned and glared.

It suddenly had second thoughts. "Sit," it ordered us. "All three. Sit and do not move."

We sat on the floor, surrounded by our guards. "Are you okay, Ken?" Amira asked. Ken grunted and kept holding his nose. His leg had started to bleed onto the floor.

I watched two struthiforms drag the ghost away.

"Up now," a struthiform ordered, prodding us with an armored foot.

"We need medical attention," I said.

"You will get it at your destination. There are no medical facilities for your kind aboard." It shoved us forward again. "Move now."

We were hustled down a ramp and into a jumpship with five struthiform guards and a carapoid pilot.

"They're bringing someone else aboard," Ken said, trying to stand up.

"One of the others survived?" A bit of hope lit up in me as I looked for a familiar face under the lump of gray being rushed in by two struthiforms.

And then I recognized the tattered, alien form, even despite the tubes and cocoons of alien medical technology wrapped around its core.

"It's Shriek," I said. And even though the face was alien, burned and jagged, I was glad to see it.

One of the other struthiforms turned to regard me. "You know this one?"

"A medic," I told it.

"We found the medic inside a stove surrounded by bottles of pure oxygen," the struthiform soldier said, and flared its feathers out. "So far, the medic refuses to speak to us."

I snorted.

"Nice to see *he* has medical attention," Ken muttered.

"He's Accordance," Amira whispered. "We're just human."

Minutes later we zipped out of the warship and curved over the remains of the base. I winced as I moved to better see out of the porthole. "Look out your windows," I said. "We did that. We survived the Conglomeration. Whatever happens next, whatever the Accordance does to us, remember this."

Shriek stirred on the stretcher and craned to look at us. "You didn't just survive," the strange alien said. "You destroyed them. You protected your home world. Though, I'm going to be curious what the Pcholem think about all this."

The pieces of the Conglomerate ship were spread out across the fields of lunar dirt around Icarus base. Some of them still glowed red.

31

"Do you remember me?" Vincent Anais asked.

Earth's strong pull weighed on me as I sat, handcuffed to a table in a large room near the very top of an Accordance administrative building. Through the floor-to-ceiling oval window, I could look down at Manhattan's silver skyscrapers spread out around the central cluster of Accordance structures.

"I do," I said solemnly. "Where's my drink?"

Anais rubbed puffy eyes. "I would laugh, but I was woken up and dragged out of bed. Then I was told we were all under attack, and that it might only be a matter of weeks before Earth would be overrun. I'm tired, recruit. And everything has changed."

"Twelve hours ago I was on the moon," I told him. "They put us on an Arvani-only ship. It was called a Manta. I think I saw one on a show once. They mainly go planet to planet, right? The way the other passengers acted, you'd think we had cooties, but armed Arvani officers shut them up. And I have yet to see a doctor." I raised my cuffed hands, trying to ignore the pain that came in waves.

Anais winced. "I'm sorry. It'll be soon."

"This isn't how you treat us. Not after what we *did*."

"What you did is up for interpretation." Anais looked away as he said that. His heart wasn't in it.

"Bullshit. You should be able to pull info out of the wreckage. The black boxes in our armor. The launcher. We told our stories on the way here, with weapons aimed at us."

"All the evidence will be carefully examined. Now, Mister Hart, moving on, where is Amira Singh?"

"I'm sorry, did you misplace her?" I stared right at Anais.

He sighed. "She seems to have, uh, escaped."

"Goodness gracious," I said. "In a secure facility like this she's gone missing? I don't know where she is, but seeing that Ken's still holding emergency medical sealant foam on his wound and my broken wrists are shackled to a table, I can't imagine why she'd turn down your hospitality."

"Has she said anything about her intentions as far as revealing sensitive military information found while at the Icarus base?"

I leaned in. "We caught a *ghost*. That's what this is about. You don't want her revealing what it is."

Anais bit his lip. "Devlin, let's be open here. Don't think you're the first to find out what the ghosts are. The Arvani administrators were all just given updates thirty minutes ago. In those files: updated information about ghosts. Information they didn't know about until now. They are . . . upset that this has been held from them. But Arvani top command has been dealing with this for a lot longer than you can imagine."

"And they're terrified that Amira will release this into the wild."

Anais nodded. "Things have gotten tense here since you left. Something like this would be explosive. Do you understand?"

Always trying to manipulate us, I thought. Even now, with the threat of invasion imminent. "I don't know where Amira is," I said. "But the last thing she told me was that, with the Conglomeration about to attack, she wasn't going to spend her last days in an Accordance cell; she was going to go enjoy them. I think the secret is safe with her."

Good luck, I'd told her when we'd gotten off the Arvani ship. *Don't let them drag you down,* she'd said, and squeezed my forearm.

"And what about you?" Anais asked. "Is the secret safe with you?"

Ken, I realized, they already considered loyal. But I was the other wild card. "It all depends on what's happening next," I said.

Anais waved his hand over the table. The white color faded. I looked at a cloud of rubble and rock, so far on the edge of the solar system that the sun was just a tiny pinprick. A suggestion of light, another star.

In the cold dark, shadows moved. Shapes with purpose.

The perspective whirled back. It was a feed from a fast-moving Accordance drone ghosting past the edge of a massive fleet of organic, irregular shapes. Some of them similar to the one in pieces near Icarus base.

"The Conglomerate forces are massing in the outer Oort cloud, on the far edges of your solar system and past our defenses. You repelled their beachhead, so they are planning a siege now. Accordance ships can't get in or out. They are trapped here with us. They need more recruits. Because the fight is coming to us."

A blast of energy wrenched through the dark and vaporized the drone. The image faded, leaving just the white table.

"The Arvani will move your family out of the political

camp they are currently in and to home custody in upstate New York," the Arvani on the left said. An Arvani tank had crept into the room silently while I was watching the video. I tried not to jump back slightly, thinking of Commander Zeus's slashing, armored tentacles. "If you agree to our conditions."

"I can't go home?" I asked.

"You are needed now more than you were before," said Anais. "Let us promote you to the youngest lieutenant, at twenty, in the CPF."

"I thought I was an octave," I said. "Aren't native ranks not allowed?"

Anais smiled. "We're getting concessions. A fully human officer corps. The chance to use native rank insignia across the force; we're configuring this all on the fly, but taking full advantage of Arvani fear. Let us train you more. Deploy you. Help the CPF fight the Conglomeration. Because they are coming for Earth, Devlin. They're coming for us."

"Get the cuffs off me, and get me a goddamned doctor," I told Anais.

I walked down toward the old financial district, enjoying the freedom to choose any direction, any path I wanted. I had no particular aim in mind, I just wanted to feel the sun on my skin, the breeze on my face. I wanted a hot dog with mustard, or a gyro, or a gelato, just something that wasn't optimally designed to fuel my metabolism.

The city was different now. Smaller, maybe. I'd had a change in perspective. The streets looked grubbier. Earth First tags spray painted on brick corners warned me that walking here in my grays might not be too smart.

There'd been bombings. The repacification hadn't worked. Human ingenuity prevailed as minds bent themselves to making life miserable for collaborators, civil servants, aliens. New York looked like a city under occupation: human enforcers in yellow riot gear in clusters everywhere, looking determined and tired. Armored struthiforms rumbling by on personnel carriers. Broken windows, destroyed buildings. The pockmarks of bullets on facades.

Concentration camps in New Jersey and Long Island. Livestreamed executions. Bombings. The occupation's iron grip was slipping, because the Accordance was pulling its forces into orbit to ready itself for the oncoming invasion.

And who knew how many Conglomerate double agents were already here?

Rumors said the Darkside base attack had opened negotiations between Earth First and the Colonial Administration for a cease-fire. Earth First was trying to decide which enemy to fear more: the one that occupied our world and its moon, or the one that might breed us into hungry heat shields.

I stopped walking around aimlessly and headed toward my appointment at the Empire State Building.

The whole side of the ancient structure had been repainted in Colonial Protection Forces gray with white swirls. And to my surprise, recruits in civilian clothes stood in a line waiting to get into the lobby. A line that wrapped around the block. Once processed, they'd be housed here before going to the Hamptons for selection.

People pointed at me as I walked by. The Accordance had used my image already this morning, broadcasting the story of our fight. Ken and I had become symbols of resistance. They'd left Amira out, as they didn't know what she was going to do next.

Even I wasn't sure I wanted that profile.

But I could use it.

As I stood in front of an auditorium full of wide-eyed recruits, I smiled. If we could fight and survive the Conglomeration, the threat that made Arvani shit their tanks, then we'd be a dangerous force.

The graffiti-spreading Earth First activists outside could cause trouble. But these recruits in front of me? They could turn on the Accordance and gain Earth its independence.

In time.

If we survived.

If I could help build them into the weapons we all needed to be.

I cleared my throat, and heard the sound amplified to three hundred pairs of intent eyes.

"Listen closely," I shouted. "There are many aliens out there. They come in all shapes and sizes. But if you want to survive your first encounter with the enemy, there are five aliens that you will need to spot on sight. Pay attention to me now, and you might live."

32

The hopper rattled and the green hills of upstate New York slid by the open side door. The Empire State base commanding officer had given me leave and let me borrow a hopper piloted by a newly promoted human pilot.

The Accordance was getting nervous, I thought, if they were letting us fly craft now.

I ran a hand down my uniform grays with the single red bar of command on my right shoulder.

What could I tell them about my decision to accept command and collaborate with the enemy?

I understood my father's desire to escape the occupation. I'd seen his desire to see people freed burn inside him since I was a child.

They'd hate what I represented. They would turn their back on me. It would hurt.

But that didn't mean I didn't want to see them.

In some ways, this upcoming visit might end up being the most alien encounter I'd had yet since joining the Colonial Protection Forces.

A long streak of lightning danced across the blue sky. A slow pinprick of light unfurled into a flower of fire that hung in place.

"Lieutenant," the pilot called back at me. "Did you see that?"

"That's orbital," I shouted back. "You hearing anything?"

"Chatter, nothing official." The hopper flared and slowed, spiraling down to land near a road leading into a forest. We arrived at the property my parents had just been moved to. A pair of guards at the end of the road walked toward the hopper as the skids hit gravel.

More pinpricks blossomed in the sky.

"That looks serious," the pilot shouted. "That looks really serious."

"It's probably automated Conglomerate probes against the orbital forts," I said.

"Someone just said the space station got hit. It's lost." The Accordance had refused to put protection around the creaky old human station. Not a military asset or necessity.

Gravel spat against the side of the hopper as the engines pounded at the road.

I looked down the road and bit my lip. "Take us up," I ordered. "Get me to the Hamptons."

The hopper scraped along the road and then got airborne with a screech of power.

My earpiece buzzed. I glanced at my wrist and accepted the call. Only one person would be using an unlisted contact to try to reach me.

Amira's voice filled my right ear suddenly. "Hey, Devlin, you seeing all this?"

"Where have you *been*?" I asked.

She moved past the question. "I just talked to Ken. The Accordance is mobilizing the CPF. No more shipping us off to other worlds, everything is getting set up to fight right here in our own solar system."

"You said 'us.' I thought you'd left."

"I wanted a vacation without anyone giving me orders," Amira said. "Consider it personal leave. They owe me that, after everything they've done. But as much as I hate the Accordance, Devlin, the Conglomeration is worse. You know that."

"I do," I said. "I already agreed to stay in. I've been helping recruit—"

"I know, you've been bunking down at the Empire State barracks. I'm in New Haven, coordinates in a few minutes once I pick a spot. Come pick me up."

"Yes, ma'am," I said crisply.

"Fuck you," she said conversationally. Then hesitated. "Make sure you arm up. People around here don't react well to seeing CPF."

She cut the connection. My wrist buzzed and displayed the coordinates.

The hopper curved around a foothill, and the road leading back toward my parents disappeared.

33

We fell into a buffeting storm, straps holding us secure to the benches in the craft. Outside, Saturn's horrific winds howled and tossed us around.

With each second the pressure squeezed the jumpship more. Outer armor plates pushed in hard enough to make the bulkheads groan.

"There's something out there in the dark," I shouted at everyone, yanking their attention away from the visibly distorting hull plates. "And we are part of an elite force of human fighters striking back against it. Accordance commanders might lead us, but we are a *human* fighting force."

Amira held up three fingers. Touchdown was imminent. Something exploded nearby, jerking the entire craft sideways and smacking us around. Close.

I tapped the stylized Earth and pockmarked moon on my shoulder. "We are the Icarus Corps. And we will make sure our world remains right where it is."

"Damn right," Ken said from the other side of the craft. None of us was sure how well the Accordance would support us. They were keeping their weaponry to themselves, leaving us to fighting with human guns. And if they cut and run, we probably wouldn't stand long against the Conglomeration. "So we will fight. Fight harder than the Accordance. Harder than the Conglomeration. Because they *can* be beat. And we have *everything* on the line."

"And if you think Accordance commanders expect a lot out of you, it's nothing compared to what we expect," Amira said, and made a fist. "Seal up!"

Helmets snapped into place with a hiss.

A second later the craft struck. The ramp dropped open and the interior of the craft filled with reddish, yellow storming air.

"Out."

Explosions blanketed the air above us. A full-on firefight. Arrow-shaped Stingrays darted about as they tried to pierce the crisscross lines of defensive fire, but burst apart and rolled off deep into the clouds.

The sun was a bright daystar from here. Or maybe that was a ship burning in orbit far overhead.

"Cover," Ken said. A twinkling star slammed into the side of the jumpship we'd just exited, ripping it apart. The debris sizzled and sunk into the fleshy surface under our boots.

"No way back but forward." Amira took point and started moving forward.

We stood on the surface of a Conglomerate mining facility. Large, gelatinous, the floating structure in Saturn's clouds stretched ahead of us for a mile. Treelike spines spouted flaring gas, lighting the hellish landscape randomly. Pockmarked ridges in the living hull provided hiding space for hostiles.

"Troll," Amira said, pointing into the distance. The chilling and familiar shape thudded toward us.

"Crickets," Ken reported.

"Okay." I pulled my MP9 up tight and looked around at my team in their black armor. "Let's go show them who they're fucking with."

THE
ICARUS
CORPS
WILL
RETURN.

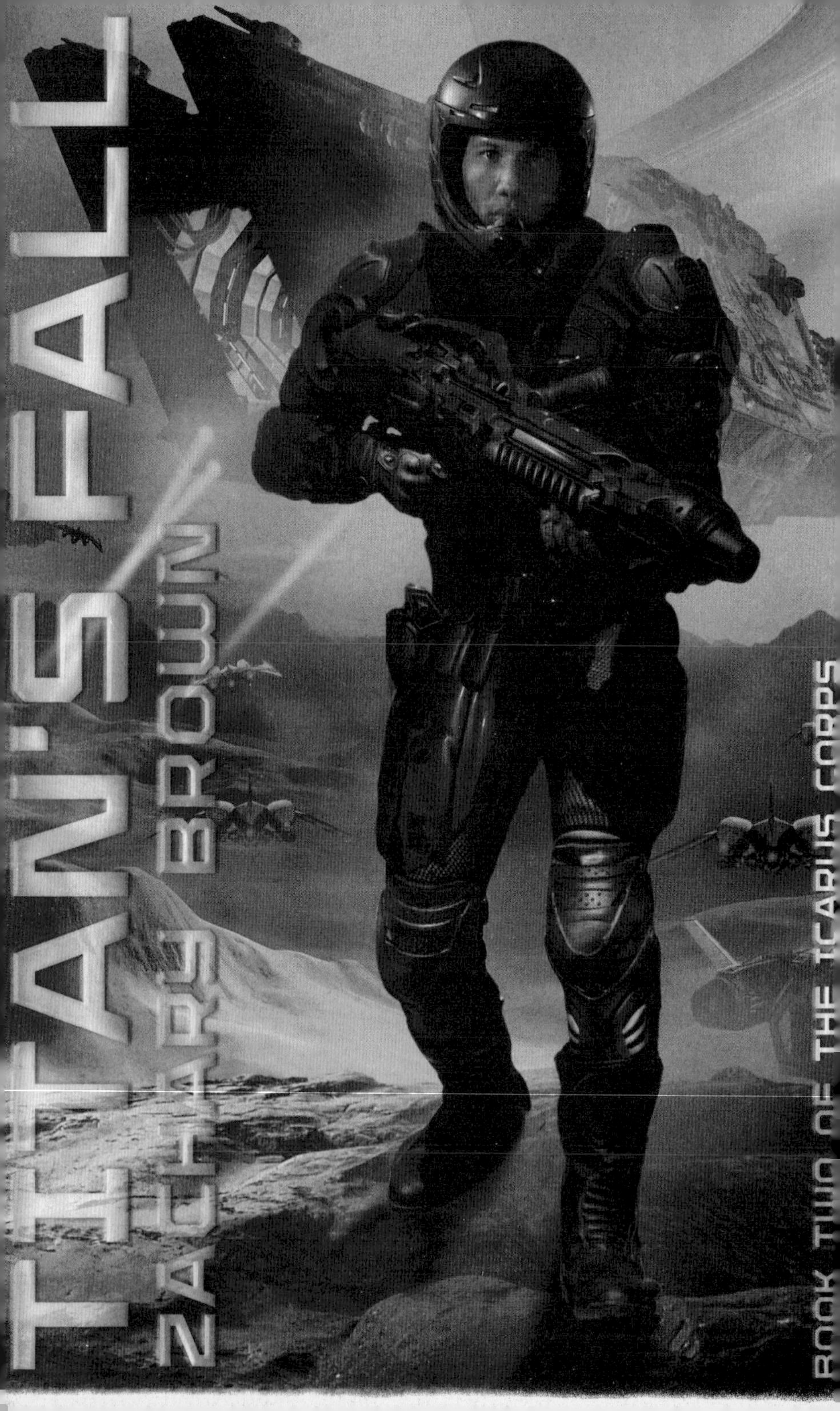
TITAN'S FALL
ZACHARY BROWN
BOOK TWO OF THE ICARUS CORPS

JUPITER RISING

ZACHARY BROWN

BOOK THREE OF THE ICARUS CORPS

SAGA PRESS

MYTHS MADE DAILY.

  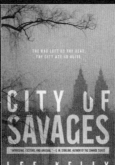 

TWO SISTERS GROWING UP
IN A POST–WWIII POW
CAMP IN MANHATTAN . . .

A HARROWING ESCAPE . . .

AND A STARTLING TRUTH
THAT WILL CHANGE EVERYTHING.

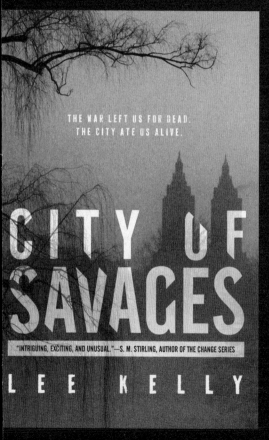

THE WAR LEFT US FOR DEAD.
THE CITY ATE US ALIVE.

CITY OF
SAVAGES

"INTRIGUING, EXCITING, AND UNUSUAL."—S. M. STIRLING, AUTHOR OF THE CHANGE SERIES

L E E   K E L L Y

In a near future where diplomacy has turned celebrity, a young ambassador survives an assassination attempt and must join with an undercover paparazza in a race to save her life, spin the story, and secure the future of her young country.

PERSONA

A RIVETING THRILLER
FROM NEBULA-NOMINATED AUTHOR

GENEVIEVE VALENTINE

PRINT AND EBOOK EDITIONS AVAILAB
SAGAPRESS.COM